ON WITH LIFE

A COLLECTION OF MEMORIES AND IMAGININGS

BY 13 WICHITA, KANSAS AND AREA SENIOR AUTHORS

ALL PROCEEDS OF THIS BOOK GO TO
SENIOR SERVICES INC. OF WICHITA, KS
A NOT-FOR-PROFIT CHARITY.

For information regarding permission, write to Starla Enterprises, Inc. Attention: Permissions Department,
375 Cedar Ranch Street, Derby, KS 67037

First Edition

ISBN: 978-1-938085-06-2

Editor & Cover Design by Starla Criser

Printed in the U.S.A.

All proceeds of this book go to
Senior Services Inc. of Wichita, KS
A not-for-profit charity

About Our Project

Starla Criser started this project in 2017. The continuing project focuses on publishing writing collections from members of the Wichita, Kansas and area senior centers.

Write On, published in 2017, is a collection of stories, memoirs, and poems from 23 Wichita area authors.

Write Again, published in 2018, is a collection of stories, articles, memoirs, and poems from 29 Wichita area authors.

Daring to Share, published in 2019, is a collection of poetry, thoughts, and short stories from 35 Wichita area authors.

On a Roll, published in 2022, is a collection of memories and imaginings including poetry, sketches, memories, and short fiction from 15 Wichita area authors.

On the Road Again, published in 2023, is a collection of poetry, sketches, memories, and short fiction from 14 area authors.

All the collections are available online at Barnes & Noble and Amazon. They are also in the Wichita library.

CONTENTS

Writing Challenges

Many of the authors in this collection belong to a group of senior adults who get together monthly for writing classes, to network, and to support each other. Some authors have used part of the exercises we do in the creation of their project(s). The words do not all have to be used or can be used in another form.

WORDS: cactus – pilot – bedroom – doughnut – screaming eagle
WORDS: leprechaun – spider – goulash – giggle – orange
WORDS: cupid – eggplant – gopher – sing – green
WORDS: fireman – cake – turtle – talk – green
WORDS: artist – pancake – poodles – cough – pumpkin
WORDS: troll – candy – skunk – yellow – gasp
WORDS: snowman – chili – pony – cried – red
WORDS: bear – blue – pizza – laugh – ballerina
WORDS: dragon – radish – caterpillar – fog – blue
WORDS: teacher – bacon – penguin – yell – white
WORDS: cowboy – liver – rabbit – chuckle – blue
WORDS: dad – chicken – alligator – whisper – black
WORDS: clown – grapes – tiger – hiss – peach

PROMPT: Write about my favorite thing to do as a child.
PROMPT: Start a sentence with "I wanted to eat everything…"
PROMPT: Write about a picnic, kids and chaos.
PROMPT: Write about a day in the life of a zoo animal.
PROMPT: Write about the life of a pet from their perspective.
PROMPT: Write about memorable family vacations.
PROMPT: Pick a Christmas song title and write a story from it.

7

JUST FUN

What You Want and What You Get Are Two Different Things!

Don Boldea

I still want to be an <u>artist</u>, but I have no artistic talent.

I still want to be a chef, but I can't even cook a <u>pancake</u> without scorching it.

I still want to be an exotic dog groomer, but I'm allergic to <u>poodles</u>.

I still want to be a doctor, but I still can't say <u>cough</u> without laughing out loud.

I still want to be a <u>pumpkin</u> pie maker, but instead I turned out to be a three-hundred-pound pumpkin eater named Peter.

I still do not want to grow old, but I am still growing old.

As the saying goes, sometimes: What You Want And What You Get Are Two Different Things!

Inspiration: This was written as part of a writing exercise using the words artist, pancake, poodles, cough, *and* pumpkin.

A Day in the Life of Charlie
E. L. Morrow

My name is Charlie. I live in a two-story house with a screened-in front porch and a fenced-in side and back yard. I live with two two-legged creatures named Mom and Dad, or Mommy and Daddy, and another four-legged creature who is something like me (more about him later).

The two-legged creatures are especially helpful for opening doors to let us out, opening the doors to let us back in, giving us food, water, and sometimes making the thing called a car to take us places. They also pet us, throw those round bouncy things called balls, and give us treats. As a group, the two-legged ones are called "people."

I said my name is Charlie, but I also answer to several other names. Names like boys, guys, and dogs. When we take walks, sometimes my people will meet other people who ask, "Is that a Corgi?" I think that means they can pet us and not be eaten. The answer is always yes, or sometimes my people say, "Yes, he's a Welsh Pembroke Corgi like the Queen used to have." After those things are said, I almost always get petted. I think Corgi means "a dog that you can pet, who does not eat children."

My people have other names for me. One of them is simply "come." When they say that, I go where they are and seem happy about it; sometimes they pet me and say "Good dog" or "Good come when you are called", and sometimes they give me treats, other times they open the door to the house or car. I am also called big boy, smart boy, but my favorite name is "Good Boy." When I'm called Good Boy, I know I will be petted, or given treats, and that I'm not in trouble for anything. Oh, I have one other name—"Out from under the table."

Well, I said I'd tell you about the other four-legged who lives in my house. He has lots of names. When he first came to live with us, he was called Down, Get Down, Back, Get Back, Stay Down, Stray Back, and Come Back Here. He is also called No Teeth. My people have given up calling him most of those names, but he's still called No Teeth once in a while. When things are going well, and he is learning the rules of this house, he gets called Coco, or Smart Boy, or even Good Boy. Even though Good Boy is my name, it's okay because I know it means I'm doing a good job teaching him how to be a Corgi in this house.

Well, you asked me to tell you about an ordinary day. I think a day is from when my people start getting up until after dark when they go back to bed. Of course, even though I am asleep, I'm never off duty. I have jobs to do all the time. For example, sometimes I will be asleep, but I know something has changed: many times, it's the monster that lives under the house. It must be a good monster, or at least my people have made it tame. The monster breathes through holes in the walls or floors. I know it's a monster because there are cages over the holes so it can't get out, and I know it's tame because it always breathes warm breath when it's cold outside, and cool air when it gets really hot outside. Well, sometimes for no reason I can tell, the monster stops breathing, and the lack of sound wakes me up. If I'm really concerned that maybe the monster is sick or something, I will bark once. Usually, Daddy will say, "It's just the air. It's okay. Go back to sleep."

As I said, I work all the time, but when we start the day, my most important jobs start up. First, I check on my people to make sure they are well and getting up. I also check on Coco. Whoever gets up first opens his kennel so I can start his lessons for the day. Next is the front door. We have to go out and check the front porch and the yard, including all the fences and gates. We check to see what animals have been in our yard: cats, the small dog down the street, opossums, birds or other unknowns. We can't keep them out when we are inside, but we pee on their scents, so they know we disapprove.

Next, we come in and have breakfast, or as our people say, Dog food in the dish. As soon as breakfast is over, we begin figuring out which of our jobs we will need to do today. We do this by watching what our people are doing. If Mom or Dad starts getting papers together, putting things in a basket, or putting on coats when it is cold, we know they are going somewhere. The next question is whether we are going with them or staying home. If they get our leashes and collars out or say something like, "Let's get in the car," or "Do you want to go for a ride?" We know that it will be a good day with possibly some treats or snacks, or even a walk in the park.

But if our people are getting ready to go and they say something like, "It's too hot," or "It's too long," or "It's too cold," we know we will have to stay home and "Guard the house." Guarding the house is another one of our jobs. We usually get a guard-the-house treat, but that is not the same as going.

When we guard the house, one of us stays at the front door, and one at the back door. I usually stay at the front door because it is the most important. No one has ever stolen the house while our people are away. Sometimes, a two-legged creature will bring a package and leave it on the front porch, or our mail friend will leave things in the box outside the porch. When that happens, we tell our people when they get home.

My most important job is keeping my people safe. My people are either very brave or very stupid; I can't tell which. I hear and smell other two-legged creatures coming down the street with one or more four-legged creatures, so I bark to let my people know there is danger, but they say, "Don't be so rude." I hope that means they are unafraid of those creatures. But just to be sure, I bark each time it happens, unless it's nap time. When it is nap time, I'm not supposed to bark unless it's a person with a package, or someone who knocks on the door.

Another important job is getting my people active. If it were up to them, they would spend all day sitting and looking at one of their boxes. One has little buttons for them to play with, another one sometimes makes a noise, and voices come out of it, but the biggest one has pictures and voices of lots of people. Sometimes there are even dogs or other animals in that box, but they never come out to play with us. I don't know why they like those boxes so much; you can't eat them, they don't roll around and play or go for walks or anything fun.

Well, as I said, we have to get our people up and doing something. This is where it really is helpful to have a little brother. Together we can convince them to bounce balls or go out in the yard to play with a bigger ball or play chase—my favorite game. We used to take walks every day until Mom and Dad started complaining about their knees and ankles hurting so much. They like the walks or games when they get started. We like it too because at the end we get a "good game treat or a good walk treat."

My other job is teaching my little brother the rules for our house. When he first came, he didn't know any of the rules. He soon got the name No Teeth, because he would play using his teeth, and sometimes he would hurt Dad or Mom. He had never lived with another dog, so he does not know how to share. When he came, he didn't know what a ball was—he thought we were supposed to eat them. He also didn't know how to eat dog food; he only wanted treats, and my people say treats are special. He is learning fast. He still has trouble sharing a ball, and he wants to be alpha dog—that's not happening; I'm alpha dog.

We do our jobs during the day. Then, when it gets dark or 4:30 pm, we get supper. Then, our people sometimes play another game with us, or they sit down to watch the big box with pictures. Sometimes, it plays music that we like, so we sing along. Along the way, usually Daddy will take us outside to check the yard and fences one more time and do whatever else we need to do. We run around the shed and fire pit, and then up on the porch. Dad or Mom locks the porch doors, and we go in to get "go to bed treats." Then we ride up with Dad in the elevator and get one final Milk-Bone when we are in our beds for the night. Little brother still sleeps in a kennel, but I have a bed and can roam the house if I hear something wrong.

When I was a puppy, I had a big brother named Winston. He loved me from the moment he saw me, and I learned a lot from him. He had to go away, and for a while, I was the only dog. When Coco was brought home, I wondered if maybe I wasn't good enough, but Daddy told me, "We got him for you so you will have someone to play with and teach." I'm just trying to be as good a big brother as the one I had.

Mom, Dad, Winston, and I went on a long trip. We had to spend the night in different rooms called motels. We got to one place where we stayed for four nights, and other people came and stayed with us. They were named Steve, Kathern, and Shamus. We slept in the room with Mom and Dad. But we roamed the whole place and went out and met other dogs (but they didn't come out).

Winston had an oozing thing on his front leg. It kept getting bigger and smelled bad. Mom and Dad took him to our Vet's office. They said it was not good. I thought they might do an operation, like they did on my legs when I was a puppy, but that did not happen. Mom and Dad wrapped the oozy spot.

After we got back from our long trip one day, Mom and Dad took Winston and would not let me go. They were gone all morning, and when they got home, they were crying. They spent most of the day petting me and talking quietly to me and each other. That night, when we went to bed, they took Winston's bed out of the room where we all slept.

I went to sleep. It seems wrong that Winston was not there. I had not been away from him at night ever since I came to live here, except when I had to be in the vet hospital with my legs. After I got to sleep that night, Winston came and told me he had to go away, and I was not the one who had to take care of Mommy and Daddy. He said, "Make them get up every day, get them to play ball, and take you on walks. You have to keep them active—that's your job now." Then he said he had to go, and I said, "No, don't go," and I cried as he left. Daddy heard me cry and got down on the floor next to my bed and said, "I miss him too. He loved you, and we love you, and we will never forget him." Dad stayed with me until I went to sleep.

The next day, I had an appointment with the Vet. As soon as we got out of the car, I knew Winston was there. I tracked his scent all the way into the building and into a big room that usually only had cats. I followed Winston around the room and then to one spot on the floor, where he stayed—but he wasn't there. Daddy was still holding my leash. I looked at him. He had tears in his eyes. He knew I knew—that is what big brother meant when he said he had to go away.

I've been back there several more times. Each time his scent is less until finally it's not there at all. Dad, Mom, and the Vets are good people. They would do only what was best for Winston. They loved him as much as I do. They rescued me from a big dog that I thought would want to play but wanted to hurt me, and from the pool when I fell in, swam from side to side, but couldn't get out.

My people have been good to me, so I am going to try to keep them getting up and going. When Daddy told me he got Coco for me, I could hear Winston saying, "You need to guide him, and love him like I did you." So that's what I am doing: being the best Corgi I know how, every day.

Inspiration: Written as part of a writing exercise to describe the life of a pet from their perspective.

A rushing stream in the Teton mountains of Wyoming.

The Ballerina
Starla Criser

Kansas summers stunk in Patty's opinion. Not just because of the gazillion percent humidity or the thousand degrees reached by late afternoon. Of course, she might be exaggerating a tad, but just a tad.

She leaned back against the rock wall of her cave in the zoo's grizzly <u>bear</u> enclosure. Unlike the zoo visitors, who were clearly sweating as they passed by, she didn't sweat. She cooled down by panting or seeking relief in shade or water. Right now, walking across the mostly dirt ground to the small pond in the middle of her space seemed like it would take too much energy.

Cloudy days were nice. Today wasn't one of them. The vast sky was bright <u>blue</u>. Pretty, but not cooling or restful.

A smell drifted her way on the non-ending breeze, one that made her nose wiggle as her brain attempted to determine the smell. Something spicy, something meaty. She sat up straighter and looked toward the three teenagers standing by the surrounding fence. One of them held a slice of <u>pizza</u>. Part of it slid from his grip to the sidewalk, making him grumble in disgust and his friends <u>laugh</u>.

Patty would like to lick up that wasted pizza and savor the taste. But that would take too much effort to walk clear over there. And she wouldn't be able to get to it, anyway.

She slumped back against the rock wall and her heavy eyelids drifted shut. Maybe a little nap would help.

Within in minutes, she fell into one of her favorite dreams. Having seen a little girl dressed one day in a flouncy pink tutu, Patty had wanted one herself. She dreamed of being a skilled, light on her feet <u>ballerina</u>. Considering she weighed around a thousand pounds and stood just over 7 feet tall, all it could ever be was a dream. Such a wonderful one, though. She sighed in delight, seeing herself spin and leap about with grace.

Inspiration: This was written as part of a writing exercise using the words bear, blue, pizza, laugh, *and* ballerina.

Witches and Goblins
C. Holden

Witches in short britches, now that is a scary sight.

They fly around the room, sometimes without a broom.

When they fly at night, now that is a scary sight.

Ghosts are another scary sight.

They like to jump out to scare you at night.

Goblins are Goblins.

Let's just leave it at that.

Coco the Corgi
E. L. Morrow

My name is Coco, and this is my story. When I was a puppy, I went to live with a couple of two-legged creatures. One of them was named Chanel (that's why she named me Coco so that it would be Coco Chanel. That means something to two-legged ones, but I don't get it). The other was named Ant. I don't understand why someone would be named after a small creature that lives under the porch, but that is what she was called.

It was clear to me that the people (another name for the two-legged) needed someone to get them organized. I guess that was why they got me. They lived in a square house in an area with lots of other square and rectangular houses called mobile homes.

I soon became the king of the house. I could run anywhere I wanted, I slept in the big bed, and I ate whatever I wanted. They tried to feed me some icky-tasting food, but I wouldn't eat it, so they gave me tasty treats. Even though I was the king, the people still wanted me to do some things their way.

They wanted me to walk outside to do my piddles and poops. Sometimes I would, but it was embarrassing with the world watching, so I usually did it on paper in the house, when no one was looking.

Most days, Chanel would leave me to go to something she called work. I didn't like it, so I would make her give me treats before I would let her back in the house. And nobody was allowed to touch me—I would bite anyone who tried. It took time, but I finally had everyone trained. My life was good. I was king. Things went on this way for most of a year.

Then one day, Chanel took me to the dog park. I liked the dog park, where I could run without a leash. But on this day, Chanel talked to some other two-legged creatures, while I ran with their dog. He looked a lot like me, only a little bigger. Then, when we went back home, these people followed in their car, and they loaded my kennel and other stuff in their car and *took me with them*. I figured it was a trip, or maybe I needed to teach these people how to treat a king.

It was clear that these people needed me. The other dog (I found out his name is Charlie) seemed to be happy with the way they did things. As soon as we got to their house, they unloaded all my things and let me outside into the dangerous world without a leash. Charlie trotted over to some grass and did his piddles and poops. Then he took me all over the yard, and it was fenced in just like the dog park. I found out these people would let us out into the yard, as they called it, without even coming with us.

They offered me food like I had had at home, and Charlie ate his immediately. I turned up my nose at mine and waited to be given treats. No treats were offered. So, I did what had always worked before: I started barking. But instead of giving me treats to get me to stop making noise, these people got out a water bottle and squirted me in the face. I barked more, and they squirted more. I barked and ran away, and they chased me with the squirt bottle. I finally stopped barking, and they said, "Good boy."

When I was called "good boy" at my home, I would get treats, but they still didn't give me any treats. After another day, I was hungry and decided to try the dry dog food they offered, and you know, it wasn't half bad. Then that evening, the people gave both me and Charlie treats. They had treats all along but wouldn't give me any until I ate the other food. Now that's just mean.

I noticed Charlie would jump up on the couch next to the people, and they would pet him, and even use a brush on him, and he didn't bite them. In fact, he seemed to like it. It took several days before I would let them pet me. I finally tried it, and you know it didn't hurt. In fact, I didn't feel like biting anybody.

They put my kennel in a room downstairs and expected me to stay there all night. Well, I whined, cried, or barked every time I heard anyone moving around the house all night. I must have finally fallen asleep. After a few nights, they moved my kennel to the room where they were sleeping. And you will never believe this; *Charlie was already sleeping there.* Not only did he sleep in their room, but Charlie had his own bed (not a kennel) and was free to move around the room, get up on their bed, have a drink of water, even push the door open and go into the hallway.

Charlie was not being treated like a king, but he was being treated like an alpha dog. Well, I decided if I'm not going to be king, at least I must be the top dog.

So, there was only one thing left for me to do: I had to prove to Charlie that I was the alpha dog, and he was my inferior. So, when we were outside at night, I raced Charlie to the porch to get back in the house first. First, I let him win, then I would give myself a head start, and somehow, he would still get there first.

Charlie taught me this game he played with another dog. We run around the shed. First, he chases me until he catches me, then I chase him, but somehow, I never catch him. I get close, and then he turns and *catches me.* I tell him that's not fair, but he tells me that's how the game is played. Since I have never lived with another dog before, I guess that must be right, but when do I get to catch him?

After I had been in this new place for about a week, Chanel and her boyfriend came to see me. I thought they were going to take me back, but they brought the rest of my stuff: more blankets and toys. There was a game I played with the boyfriend. He would slap me on the side of my face, but I could always nip his hands before he could get away. After they left, I decided to play the game with "Daddy" (Daddy is another name for one of the two-legged ones.) Well, when I tried to bite his hand instead of playing the game, he said, "NO." I don't like that word, so I tried again, and do you know what he did? He grabbed my mouth with both hands and said, "No, no, no, no" a lot of times while he was shaking my snout. He made me feel bad. I wanted to go home with Chanel and her boyfriend, where I was king, and I could bite and nobody got mad.

I was sad for a whole day. Charlie came and sat with me and said, "I guess you are going to be here from now on." I realized that that was okay. Most of the time, I liked where I was. The people are kind. I like playing with Charlie, being petted, and running in the yard.

There is one more thing about this house that is so different. They have these little round creatures that the people pick up. After they pick them up, the creatures jump out of their hands and bounce off the wall or floor, and Charlie grabs them and then gives them back to the people. The first time I got one, I wanted to be sure it was dead, so I slung the life out of it, and Charlie got upset with me because I wouldn't give it back to the people. Apparently, the two-legged ones make them come back to life, so they jump around again.

The people call those round things "balls." When they say that word, my big brother gets all excited. There is one special ball Daddy calls "the talking ball." It makes wha-wha noises when it rolls. When anyone says, "talking ball," Charlie goes to the special drawer where it lives and tries to open it. We always play with it outside on the driveway. The people throw it, and we chase it. Charlie always gets it; my mouth is too small to get hold of it. The people also have a smaller one that does not talk, which I can catch. But Charlie likes to get that one too, just so I will have to tug on it with him.

I try not to let him know, but Charlie seems to be just a little bit better at most things than me. So, there is only one way left to show that I am the alpha dog. So, I jump on his back to make him kneel to me, and he just smiles and walks out from under me, leaving me flopping down on the floor. I suspect I will have to let Charlie think he is top dog until he gets older and slows down.

Now we go on walks just to see people, and I like taking rides in the car— sometimes we get treats, or even French fries. I am no longer king, but I like my new home, and I like playing with Charlie, even if he thinks he is the alpha dog. I realize I could have been nicer to Chanel and the boyfriend, or even the ant. They did everything they knew to help me be happy. I hope they find a pet that can make them happy.

I'm a little more than two years old. I have been the king, and now I'm almost the top dog. I've learned a lot from Charlie and our people. It is nice for now not to have to be in charge of everything. They take care of us and protect us. It feels good to just be the youngest for now. I can let Charlie pretend to be the alpha dog and my big brother for a while.

Inspiration: Written as part of a writing exercise to describe the life of a pet from their perspective.

My Day in the Zoo as an Elephant
David Larimore

Wow, who would have thought I'd be so popular for doing NOTHING. For just being born. After all, isn't every animal born? They don't make such a big deal every time a prairie dog is born. And have you seen the prairie dog area? There are dozens of babies over there, wrestling with each other and playing hide-and-seek or tag as they dart in one hole and out another. It looks like a giant *whack-a-mole game* over there, ya never know when a head will pop-up.

Well anyway, I'm one of the four new baby elephants at the Sedgwick County Zoo. Hundreds if not thousands of humans of all ages come stare and point at me daily. Yep, I'm pretty popular. I walk about with my mom or my aunties, and the humans try to guess which one is my mom. But then I see several human moms whisper the answer to their kiddos. "See the baby elephant lift up its trunk and push its mouth up between that big elephant's front legs? The baby is nursing … getting milk from that one, so that one is its momma."

Why are they whispering? It's not a secret or embarrassing to nurse in public … and I am inspired by that ol' saying, 'MILK, it does a body good.'

Maybe they should paint a black stripe on me, like the zebras. That would help spectators know which baby elephant I am. Ya see, spectators often call me by the wrong name. Some yell, "Hi Bomani," while others yell, "Hi Kijani," or "Hi Asali," or "Hi Dakari," … but that's okay, just don't call me Late for dinner. Ya see, I'm a growing boy, and I want to grow up big and strong like my dad. Although as of last week they still haven't let Bull-Elephant Dad come out and teach me how to play ball or whatever games elephants play.

Speaking of eating to get big, they feed me hay and leaf-covered branches. I heard the zookeepers talking about a zoo that fed a live chicken to their

<u>alligator</u>. I'd probably run from the chicken, like I ran from the Canadian goose that chased me.

Anywho, I hope you bring friends and family to the Sedgwick County Zoo to see all the animals.

Inspiration: This is written using the exercise words *dad, chicken, alligator, whisper,* and *black* along with writing about a day in the life of a zoo animal.

A Most Unusual Friendship
Starla Criser

Stefano gave a squeaky greeting as he ambled down the riverbank toward his friend. It made him smile when Timothy looked up from his favorite sitting spot under the bridge, his big brown eyes lighting up in delight.

Then he stood up, forgetting how tall he was and how he had been sitting under the shorter part of the bridge. He conked his head and grumbled something Stefano didn't understand but imagined wasn't anything happy.

"It's been too long," Timothy said, rubbing his head. "I've missed talking to you."

Stefano settled himself on a patch of grass, curling his bushy black-and-white tail around him. "The Fam has had a lot of visitors lately. The kids like to show me off. Try to get me to do a few tricks they think they've taught me. Like rolling over or some other ridiculous thing to reward me with an egg or a <u>yellow</u> jacket."

Timothy gave a nod of understanding, of sympathy. "Still, you like your Fam. Like your cushy home."

Stefano couldn't deny it. A couple of years back, the kids had found him as a baby <u>skunk</u>, sitting lost and frightened beside his dead mother. Some idiot driver had hit her as they'd been crossing the road in front of their farm. They'd taken him home, had him fixed so he couldn't spray, and built him a pretty nice pen to live in. He liked his humans, but he liked to sneak away for an adventure or to visit his friend whenever he got a chance. He'd had that opportunity today.

He glanced around, sniffed a bit, wondering if there were any grubs close by. That was how he'd met Timothy. Stefano had been wandering around this bridge, looking for some grubs to eat that day.

He remembered how Timothy had slipped on a muddy stone in the water under the bridge. He'd scared Stefano so much he'd <u>gasped</u> and nearly had a heart attack. But Timothy had looked so unhappy with his situation that Stefano had scooted closer and asked if he was hurt.

Timothy had looked stunned that anyone, even a skunk, had actually seen him. He was a <u>troll</u>, after all, and only believed to be mythological. Except he wasn't. He was real. From that odd moment on, they'd become friends. The troll who nobody seemed to notice living by this river and under the bridge. And the skunk who most humans and animals kept their distance from.

"I've got treats," Timothy said in his usual deep voice. "Some recently washed pebbles for me, and some dead crickets that I found the other day and saved for you."

Stefano scurried closer. "Crickets! Yum!" He grinned at his friend. "And your <u>candy</u> of choice: pebbles."

As soon as Timothy brought forth his stash of goodies, they settled down to eat and share the latest news in their lives.

Inspiration: This was written as part of a writing exercise using the words troll, candy, skunk, yellow, *and* gasp.

The Dragon and the Caterpillar
Starla Criser

Once upon a time, in a land far away, lived a <u>caterpillar</u> named Matilda. She knew her life would change all too soon, and it was scary just thinking about it. She liked living in her bush and had a favorite branch she crawled up and down. She couldn't imagine not doing this anymore.

As she opened her eyes this morning, there was a strange <u>**fog**</u> in her forest. She could barely see to the end of her branch. If she moved too fast, she feared she would lose her balance and fall off. So, she dug her tiny, tiny feet into the branch and tried to stay as still as she could.

Suddenly, the world around her seemed to shudder, shake, vibrate. She struggled not to move, but it was hard. What was happening? "Oh, make it stop!" she cried out, afraid no one could hear her soft voice.

It happened again. The earth beneath her tree shook. Her tree shook as well. She fought hard not to lose her grip on her branch. If she fell to the ground… Well, she didn't even want to think about what might happen.

Then she saw what was causing all the turmoil in her world. It was that silly <u>blue</u> <u>dragon</u> who had recently appeared in her forest. He wasn't as big as some dragons she'd seen. Really only the size of a bush, but he had long, bird-like wings and fluttered about recklessly. Like now. One of his wings hit her tree. Hit the branch she was clinging to.

She fell right onto his head, onto his nose. She dug in her small feet and glared at him, right in his startled eyes. Even though he couldn't hear her, she gave him a piece of her mind. "Look what you've gone and done! You've knocked me off my branch!" She pulled in a breath and continued, "If I'd fallen to the forest floor, you would have trampled me, no doubt!"

He crossed his golden eyes and looked at her. Then he smiled goofily, amused with what he'd done. Silly dragon!

While she tried to figure out how to keep hanging onto him, he opened his mouth. He didn't shove out his long tongue to lick her, thank the stars! But as he drew in a breath, a weird smell overcame her. Something like a <u>radish</u>, maybe. A knight riding through the forest not long ago had been chomping down on one, and it had smelled just awful.

"Please put me back where I belong," she quietly pleaded, not expecting him to understand.

To her surprise, he smiled again. Before she could get a better grip on his nose, he fluttered up higher. He stopped mid-air right next to her favorite spot and cocked his head. Enough to cause her to slip sideways and land exactly where she wanted to be.

As she regained her hold on the branch, he shifted away and smiled once more. "Sorry, m'lady," he said, "didn't mean to bother you."

With that, he flew away, leaving her shocked that she'd heard him. Life could certainly be strange sometimes. At least she was back where she belonged.

This was written as part of a writing exercise using the words dragon, radish, caterpillar, fog *and* blue.

The Leprechaun Legend
Don Boldea

<u>Leprechauns</u>, yes they do exist! Let me tell you I know they exist. These small, mischievous and agile fairies, or nimble goblins, supposedly exist only in Irish folklore. But Nooooo, that's not true.

First, they are short and all of them are decked out in a green colored suit topped off with a large green brimmed pilgrim type hat to cover their <u>orangey</u> red hair and beard. Out of their bowl of <u>goulash</u> their bearded shaggy face extends a long stemmed pipe. What's more, their chilling <u>giggle</u> just adds to their ghoulish demeanor.

Supposedly they are cobblers who create stylish footwear for the other ferries of their kind. They work in a dark, small and <u>spider</u> infested cave like room. In the attached workroom is also where they hide many types of their treasures. However, they are also protectors of a huge pot of gold. It's said if a mere mortal catches a leprechaun, for his freedom he will offer up where his pot of gold is hidden.

The legend of these leprechauns may have their beginnings in Ireland, but it's a myth that they exist only in Ireland. In the United States every March 17th we celebrate those same little mythical goblins on St. Paddy's Day. In addition, our celebration consists of a large consumption, I mean a sensible amount of consumption of green beer; the wearying of a four-leaf clover shaped badge; enjoying parades; wearing something green or you'll feel the Irish pinch; and carrying large signs that yell out, "Kiss Me I'm Irish!" Of course everyone must talk about how we would like to capture a leprechaun and find his pot of gold.

That's the true story of the Leprechaun Legend.

Please note this one final message. It's almost too generous, but! As it happens if you want to capture your own leprechaun and enjoy his pot of gold I'm offering just the thing. I'm selling the real one and only one of a kind Leprechaun Pot of Gold Snare. Just look for the rainbow prominently over the black pot of gold, it signifies it's your guarantee!

This fabulous fifty percent off, one of a kind offer, for the Leprechaun Pot of Gold Snare, is only $19.99. Be the first in your neighborhood to reel in the never-ending riches of Leprechaun's Gold!

Supply is limited so only two per order is accepted please. This offer ends soon, hurry send your cash, money order or cashier's check from a recognized bank for only $19.95, free delivery included, and you'll receive your Leprechaun Pot of Gold Snare today and soon you'll being lavishing in the never-ending riches of Leprechaun's Gold!

Inspiration: This was written as part of a writing exercise using the words leprechaun, goulash, spider, giggle, *and* orange.

31

REMEMBERING

Am I There Yet?

(Unsent letter to my granddaughter and prologue to my memoir)
Nancy Breth

Thank you, dear Kayla, for checking in with your old grandma today. What a sweet surprise on this gray and dreary day. So glad to hear you have reached another milestone—paying off your car! You sounded so excited about your new job and your new life in Kansas City. Yet still you seemed perplexed and a little disappointed that you still had not found your passion. You said you still felt unfulfilled.

Dear Granddaughter, I know so well that persistent and demanding voice inside asking, "Am I *there* yet?"

Like you and almost everyone I know, we all have this nagging voice that keeps yelling at us, *"When are you ever going to get there?"* And even though, for me, that voice has gotten softer and quieter through the years, it has never gone away for good. But I have learned that it is okay for me, because it just means I will always want to be changing, growing; not giving in to standing still.

I ask myself am-I-there-yet questions several times a week. "Am I living the life that I want?" "Have I fulfilled all of my dreams?" "Will I ever feel completely at peace with who I have become?" Even though I am 78 years old as I am finishing this letter.

And every time I sit down to work on stories for my memoir, I am asking myself questions about my life. Why am I writing a memoir? Do I want people to revere and remember me? Is it to pass on some bits of wisdom to my loved ones, hoping that they won't make some of the same stupid mistakes I did? Or is it about letting people inside my life to know me better—this woman who is so quiet and private?

I confess it is a bit of all of these. But today, hearing your mild disappointment amid all the new and exciting happenings you were telling me about, I know why I have kept at writing this collection of short stories.

This memoir is for me to remember those moments I realized I had been *there,* right where I always longed to be—*always.* I just couldn't see that at the time.

As a mother, there were so many times I remember thinking, *When am I ever going to feel like a good mother?* Thinking that once Carrie and Marty were both potty-trained, I could feel like I was being a good mom and enjoy the kids more. Or in those teen years when I could do nothing right to make them both happy—I thought maybe when they were out on their own we would have a better relationship, and I wouldn't feel like such a failure.

In wanting to hurry them along to the next step, I lost a lot of time trying so hard to be this perfect vision of what a mother *should* be, when I could have been enjoying those special (and sometimes very messy and very irritating) moments of each day that came and went so quickly.

The kids and I had a better relationship after they left home. A special Mother's Day trip across Texas with them helped remind me why that is. I would always get so furious with them when we were on road trips together in their younger days. They would tease each other and whine "Are we there yet?" all the way to our destination even though they knew it irritated me.

The beginning of our trip across Texas began at Marty's home in Corpus Christi. He drove us to our first stop, the casino in Eagle Pass, which is on the border of Mexico. All the way there, the three of us were teasing each other, taking turns whining, "Are we there yet?" "Are we there yet?" And we were laughing so hard, we had to make a pit stop at each small town we encountered on that desolate highway through desert-like cattle ranches.

That trip, the three of us spending several days driving to several destinations across the big state of Texas, reminded me that on all those road trips we took when the kids were still living at home, I could have chosen to just enjoy the ride. Instead, I almost always had this "I must make my kids be perfect to be a good mother" agenda. I could have laughed heartily instead of stressing out. And could have "seen" my kids as perfect just the way they were back then. I could have enjoyed every minute like I did on this trip through Texas, just by being fully present in the moments.

There will be other travel stories in my memoir, but not much about the exotic scenery or finding treasured mementos along the way. My stories are mostly about finding treasure in the moments shared with my travel companions and with others we met along the way. *Stories of the Wow of the Now!!*

My stories are of seemingly ordinary moments that radically changed how I felt about myself and others. I spent so much of my life beating up on myself because I didn't measure up to this long-held perfect image I thought I had to be before I could feel happy and loved. These perfectly imperfect moments I will be sharing are about times I found the love and joy I was looking for right inside my heart.

Like one ecstatic moment when I became fully, deeply aware of the importance of me (as a unique and worthy-to-be-alive me). Was it after finally getting my college degree at 30 as a single mother working full time? Was it after getting the final computer up and running after being in charge of a new computer system installation that I had worked on for months?

No, it was a quiet, silent moment—just me in my car about 5 a.m. on my way to the hospital to spend the day with Carrie after her brain surgery when a stranger tried to hijack my car.

I was at a stoplight when this man appeared out of the shadows and came toward my passenger door. I ran the red light, getting away before he could get ahold of the door handle.

I can still see that man coming toward me; no other car or person in sight for miles. And I can also remember clearly how determined I was to get to the hospital before Carrie opened her eyes. Being with her through that nightmare of almost losing her was the only thing that mattered.

As I raced away from the man's grasp, my life flashed before my eyes.

And then it struck me, like a spotlight being pointed right at me. How important I was to this daughter of mine. *Me*—her mother, who knows her and loves her better than any of the team of nurses and doctors. *Me*—who she is most comfortable with, who didn't flinch seeing her head bandaged, hair sticking out—caked with blood, and the catheter slowly filling up at the foot of the bed.

You see, Dear Granddaughter, I have found through all the ups and downs of my long life that fulfillment and peace and joy are not some climaxes we are working toward where we will finally know without a shadow of a doubt that we are *there*. We find a fulfilling life by being aware of all the gifts that life offers us each and every day—and knowing how important we are in this life here and now.

Most of all, this memoir is about finding treasure in the simple things, the extraordinariness of the ordinary moments that have touched my heart and expanded this love that just keeps growing larger and stronger through the years. Moments I want to remember always. Moments I want to share with others now—to let friends and family know how much I have appreciated the times we have shared. And to maybe inspire them to be more aware of the treasure that is in full view right in front of them every minute of every day.

One treasured memory is the day you first called me "Grandma." I can still see you, dear Kayla, as you handed me this little pink plastic basket with tiny flowers on it, full of candy.

Since you were about three when I became your grandmother; it took us a while to get to know each other. You were so shy that Mother's Day when you gave me that sweet gift, but you bravely said it out loud, "Happy Mother's Day, Grandma," and made my heart sing with joy.

Another special time I will include in my memoir is our trip from Pittsburgh, Pennsylvania, to Wichita together. It is titled, "One-Way Ticket"—our trip where I flew to the Pittsburgh airport to join you in your move back to Wichita. That trip was a leap of faith for both of us. As we drove through six states in two days, we connected in a way that feels like a bond that will last forever (I hope). And we both found out how alike we are in so many ways; even though I am 45 years older than you.

Dear Granddaughter, my heart is a treasure chest filled with sweet memories, thanks to you and all my family and all my friends and the gazillions of people I have connected with in different ways in different times and places.

There have been times in my life when I seriously thought of ending my life because I believed at the time that I would never *get there*—to that place where I was at peace with who I was and felt worthy of being alive. But that was long ago. I have come a long way since those times when I was blind to the love, the joy, the peace that was mine always, every step of my journey, if only I had seen life with my heart and not my ego.

It took me a very long time to find out that joy is not a destination—a place you get to only if you get each item on your to do list done, or tackle all your goals, or become the perfect you, or find the perfect job and mate and place to live. Joy is what you find in the small and seemingly ordinary moments of your life along the way. Joy is a choice, a way of seeing the world. A choice to love and accept and be thankful for *what is*, no matter how awful it may seem at the time.

I've traveled to many states, had many fun adventures, seen mountains, oceans, magnificent views. But the most outstanding state I've been in is the state of peace.

The most magnificent views were all the smiles—first smiles from my babies, Carrie's smile through the pain when we washed her hair for the first time after her brain surgery, Marty's smile when he proudly showed me the Soapbox Derby car he finished all by himself, the smile from grandson Albert when he purposely steered our paddleboat under a fountain and we got all wet, the smile you gave me when you first called me Grandma. So many smiles in my past and so many certain to be there in my future.

This treasure box (my heart) is full to overflowing.

Am I *there* yet?

Yes indeed, I have to say—right *here* and *now*, each and every day!

And so are you, my dear Kayla, as well as everyone we know. I pray that each and every one comes to know that in their lifetime (and hopefully much sooner than I did).

Childhood Memories
Starla Criser

There were many things I liked to do as a child and many good memories. Even all those years ago, I had an active imagination, much like I do today as an author. One similarity was in creating settings to play in, like creating scenarios for my stories now. Another was that I had favorite dolls who were like the characters I create in my storylines. I even had stuffed animals who played parts in my fantasy world, like the farm animals today in my children's book series about Blossom the cow.

In my early elementary school days, that fantasy world was often inside of a house I made by draping a blanket over our dining room table. I'd crawl under there alone or with one of my best friends, Margaret or Kathy. Sometimes we'd make side rooms to our "house" by draping sheets over the chairs.

If we played outside, it was usually on my swing set. We would see how high we could swing. Sometimes I even got high enough that my feet were at the same height as the top of the swing set. We'd pretend we were flying in one of those airplanes my dad worked with in his job at Boeing. Or we'd not go quite so high, but high enough to jump out of the swing without killing ourselves. Although Mom was always sure that's just what we were going to do. Not a happy camper about that sometimes.

Other good times were when our family visited my grandpa's house in Holdrege, Nebraska. There was a family next door with kids around my age. We'd run wild all over his acreage, chasing each other round and round his house. Or playing hide and seek in his apple orchard. Or we'd play Annie, Annie, Over and toss (or try to) a ball over the house's roof to each other. Sometimes our throws weren't the greatest, but we never broke a window.

I also remember playing jacks, marbles, and Pick-Up-Sticks with my friends. Occasionally, Mom would even get down on the floor and play with me. We didn't do a lot together over the years, but there were some times that I remember and that make me smile. She had a warm heart, loved to play games, and could act like a kid at times, too. Like me. So that's another wonderful memory that I forget sometimes.

My dad, too, made life fun with his love of teasing everyone, especially Mom. Anytime we took a family picture, he almost always held up two fingers (like devil's horns) over the head of whoever he was next to. Of course, Mom got furious when she later developed the pictures. And he loved to tickle us unmercifully at times, again, especially Mom. Who would swat his arm when she managed to get away from him and say, "Stop that, Jack!" I guess that tickling issue is why I loved to do that to my daughter sometimes over the years. Still do occasionally.

When I think about winter, I remember the games we used to play in the snow. Mom would shuffle around in it until she made a big circle and two cross paths. I think we called it playing Duck, Duck, Goose. Because we'd chase each other and throw snowballs at each other. Oh! We'd make snow angels, too. Even Mom. I don't remember Dad ever doing it, but then he was no "angel."

These later memories of play times with my family were from when I was in my early teens, when my sister was around six or seven. Thinking back now, there were a lot of memories I haven't thought about in a long time.

This was written as part of a writing exercise about "my favorite thing to do as a child."

Pennies From Heaven—Symphony in GEE Major
Nancy Breth

Many days combined from walks when I lived in a manufactured home in River Oaks Mobile Home Park, Wichita, Kansas.

My daily walks are medicine for my body, mind and spirit. A habit I started many years ago that has helped me put those dark days of constantly battling Major Depressive Disorder behind me.

This morning on my walk, I spied another penny to add to my coin jar. Occasionally I find quarters, nickels or dimes or even a five-dollar bill once. I take the same routes around this mobile home park and beyond and almost always I find at least one penny each day. I like to think of these penny sightings as a sign from God of how prosperous I am.

When I first start my walk, I am usually thinking of my to-do list and beating myself up for what I haven't accomplished yet. But the more I walk, the more gifts from heaven I see in my surroundings. The more I hear the symphony of God's love calling me to come join in the joyful celebration of life.

Yesterday, my little buddy Micah made my heart sing again. He must be five or six, always wearing clothes that don't fit and most of the time no shoes. Yesterday he wore two tennis shoes way too big and on the wrong feet. But little Micah didn't care that his tiny butt crack showed when his droopy drawers almost fell off when he stood up. He gave me this big hug and said I love you and I could feel he meant it. He said he loved my hair, my jacket and my shoes.

Micah didn't care that I had left dirty dishes in the sink, or that my hair was flat on one side, and I was wearing the same outfit I had on the day before, and that I hadn't showered yet either. He loved me even though I hadn't finished one line on my to-do list yet or saved the poor or led a protest. What a gift—a hug and to know I am loved.

Today I see a preschooler—a chubby little guy whirling around in his yard. He is lost in the joy of this grand moment, dancing with the wind, the swaying of the trees, the singing of the birds. Until he sees me—a stranger, and that means danger as we teach our young ones and runs to his door. I hope he doesn't spend the rest of the day in front of the TV seeing a multitude of acts of violence before he nods off to sleep at night.

Numerous dragonflies are buzzing up and down in front of me, reflecting the sun's rays and leading me to "lift up thine eyes."

Love's music is soaring on the wings of a robin carrying his family's feast in his beak. Two turtledoves are perched on the telephone line cooing softly to each other.

The dogs I pass by one by one are announcing my arrival to their territory with a warning bark. Protecting their loved ones with their loud and angry posing that hides a soft, cuddly playfulness inside.

The leaves are dancing for me, skip-skip-clicking in brilliant reds and golds streaming across my view. The traffic on the busy street blocks away is thrum-thrum-humming a steady beat in the background.

Soon I am at the Rose Queen's corner. I don't know her name, just know she must have dementia because someone is always outside on the porch watching out for her as she works in her flower garden. Today, she looks truly regal in her long red bathrobe as she walks toward me. She has a smile that lights up her face as she says, "Baa, baa, baa."

As I listen to her speak, my heart tells me she is saying what a beautiful day it is and how happy she is to be outside tending to her garden.

I tell her how beautiful her flowers are and that she has done a great job. When she smiles back, I know she is thanking me for stopping by to say hello again, as I always do when she is out in the yard when I pass by. As she waves goodbye, I know she is hearing Love's music in her heart too.

Just down the block from the Rose Queen's, I get "love bombed." A little ball of kinky white fur, who had been running through wet grass excitedly, jumps all over me. My jeans get all muddy. But thankfully I am wearing ready-for-the-laundry-already jeans so I can laugh about it. The dog belongs to the mother and daughter who are standing by their mailbox waiting for a bus. I've seen these two before and know that the daughter has Down syndrome and goes to special education classes.

The so-excited-to-be-here daughter shouts, "How are you?"

I say, "Fine, thank you. How are you?"

She replies, "I'm good. Can I give you a hug?"

I say that I would love to have a hug. And she gives me the sweetest of hugs! Then, she buzzes back to her mother trying to talk her into letting her walk with me for a while until the bus gets there.

As I head back home, the crickets and the birds are singing so loud, I hear nothing else in the last block. The final crescendo of a Symphony in GEE! Another beautiful day to do with or *Ta Dah* with however I wish! Another day gathering up Pennies from Heaven!

Emily's Gift
Connie Holt

In her elementary school years, Emily Belle Carmichael attended Hardscrabble School, the actual name of the small school located in a rural area on the prairies of Kansas. My mother, Emily, grew up in a family of eight children, and hardscrabble pretty well described their life at the beginning of the Great Depression.

She was in the eighth grade, her final year of school, and her mom and dad purchased large pails of peanut butter and syrup to make sandwiches for their children's school lunches. Once, one of her friends came up with a game of everyone trading lunches one day a week just for fun. My mom, Emily, loved this as occasionally, she would hit the jackpot, scoring an orange or banana and maybe a ham sandwich. These were foods she rarely got to eat, but alas, soon the game was over as no one wanted to trade with Emily anymore!

The funny thing is years later she introduced us children to peanut butter and syrup sandwiches, and every one of us loved them! I still love them!

One day, her teacher announced they were going to put on a play. She would be auditioning everyone that very day. Emily had a low but melodious voice, and she loved reciting poetry and Mother Goose nursery rhymes.

After her audition, her kind teacher told her she was wonderful and would love for her to have the main part, but unfortunately, the teacher told her she knew Emily's parents could not afford the costume.

Years later, when she told us children this story, it was with no bitterness, but with a pride that her teacher recognized her talent. Then she would launch dramatically into reciting the nursery rhymes for us.

Later, when she was in a nursing home, any time small children would visit, she would use that voice to entertain them with nursery rhymes. The adults as well as the children would applaud her performance, and her smile and her blue-green eyes would light up!

A Cat Named Ruby

Ruby Tobey

My daughter lived in Mesquite, Texas, for a while. It was always a long drive, but we visited on weekends whenever we could.

Once when we were there over Sunday, we went to her Sunday school class. They introduced the visitor and named us as Maria's parents, Joe and Ruby Tobey.

After the morning worship service was over, a lady came and said to my daughter, "I about fell off my chair when they introduced your mom because we have a cat named Ruby and a dog named Tobey.

True story.

An old barn sketched near Prairie Grove, Arkansas

Dreams Never Die
Donald C. Septer

Sitting, thinking about our dreams
Those that we made for us to share
But now I'm left with only dreams
That will remain unfulfilled

Thought I no longer needed dreams
Since now I'm all alone
Then reality came knocking and I began to realize
That I had had only one dream

It was my dream and my dream alone
And I finally began to understand

That all those who had come and gone in my lifetime
Were only there to share in part of my dream

Even the time we had together

Was time we only shared in each other's dream
During that time our dreams became one
And now that you're gone so is your part of our dream

But my dream remains with me
Our dreams had fit perfectly together like pieces of a jigsaw puzzle
And as with others in my life their dream fit together with mine
Even though it was only for a short time I came to realize

That my friends, my family and you my wife
Had only been pieces of my dream
Just as my dream was a piece of yours and theirs
Now as each day as my life goes by
People will come and people will go
Each with their time and piece of my dream

On with Life: Memories and Imaginings

And now even though some are gone
And some will never return I realize this one thing

That my dream will always remain
With me as long as I live and when I'm gone
Only my part of the dream will die with me

And I now understand this one fact of life
Dreams never die only people do.

Inspiration: When I wrote this, it would have been my late wife's birthday. I was having my ups and downs. That day was more of an "up" day and I wrote this philosophical poem about my life.

A Night to Remember
Nancy Breth

April 14, 2012, 7:00 a.m.—the day of *A Night to Remember—Titanic Dinner Theater Gala*, a one-hundred-year recognition of the sinking of the *Titanic* at the Haysville Community Library was finally here!

My daughter Carrie and I had been counting the days. This evening at 5:30 p.m. we would pretend to be the wealthy Newell sisters, who boarded the brand-new steamship *Titanic* with their father to return home from a trip to the Holy Land one hundred years ago.

Our first-class tickets purchased at the library had the name, age and a brief bio of an actual person who had been aboard the *Titanic* before it sank. First-class ticket holders would be on the first floor of the library and have a seven-course meal; the steerage class would be in the basement and served Irish stew and biscuits.

I was looking forward to an evening of luxury—just one meal without beans as the main ingredient. Just one evening to enjoy the comfort and luxury of being waited on and entertained. For one evening only, I could pretend that I was headed to the Promised Land and forget about all the disasters that had happened in the last year.

Just over a year ago, my ship had fallen apart. I began sinking bit by bit. I lost my voice (sounded like I had laryngitis) as a side effect of a thyroidectomy. Then lost my job of 12 years after the owner sold the company. A disastrous divorce had blindsided my son, Marty, breaking his heart and mine and my bank account to help him out.

I had to draw Social Security at sixty-four to survive this sinking ship, which shattered my dreams of traveling during retirement. Thoughts of doom and gloom were flooding my mind every day. Almost every morning I would wake up in a panic. "What am I going to do with my life now?" I kept asking God; but wasn't hearing any answers.

Buying that first-class ticket for the *Titanic Dinner Theater Gala* instead of the steerage class was my way of saying to myself that life is good, things will get better, that I deserved a treat to cheer me up.

On April 14, 2012, 10:00 a.m. the warnings began early in the day. Massive storms headed our way and were predicted to reach us by late that evening. So that really spoiled the excitement of the day. Time to prepare for another disaster!

Tornado watches are commonplace in Kansas, and my usual reaction is to ignore them all until I hear the sirens go off and see a funnel cloud headed my way; but this massive force headed our way was especially foreboding. The weather stations were predicting with precise timing and location when and where these monstrous funnels of destruction would be next as the storms ravaged town after town throughout Nebraska, Iowa, and Oklahoma. And now this huge storm was bearing south through Kansas toward Wichita.

This was a titanic-size storm front coming, and I knew in my gut that this was going to be a night to remember. I couldn't ignore the possibility that my mobile home, my car and all my "stuff" could be blown away in an instant on this night.

I had plenty of time to pack my valuables and the few necessary items I would need if something leveled my home. It was easy deciding to pack the makeup and toothbrush, the clean change of clothes, the removable disk where I stored my photos and other computer files. But it was a struggle to decide among all the irreplaceable items what would fit into one backpack.

Without hesitation, Carrie's book of handwritten poems, *Feelings of Love*— that she made just for me for Mother's Day—went into the backpack. Her poems openly share her tender feelings of love as she was growing from a teen to an adult woman. A heartwarming, heartbreaking reminder of all the ups and downs and in-betweens she and I shared through her teenage years. An inspiring and joyful reminder of what a caring and compassionate woman she has grown to be.

The bookmark that was included in my Christmas card from Marty on the first Christmas after he and his wife separated was also tucked in with care. The bookmark has words written on it—of love and appreciation for a mother. Words that I read over and over to remind me of the deep love we share that helped us both get through the divorce and the years that followed when, together, we all adjusted to this new life he was living as a single man again.

So many precious things called out to me for attention; but I knew I couldn't take them all. So instead, I went through each room and closet, taking pictures and gathering treasured memories. Like the white ceramic dove, the green glass perfume bottle with a bird on top, the little ceramic ring holder with swans and flowers on the lid—the very first things the kids bought for me with their own money at a garage sale when they were ten and nine. No high-priced jewels that are taken out for special occasions and then locked away safe from thieves, could ever bring the joy I experienced over and over when I looked at those precious gifts and remembered how rich I felt when the kids gave me these treasures.

The tiny pink plastic flower basket that was filled with candy that granddaughter Kayla gave me the day she called me Grandma for the first time is very special to me. And also a reminder of the beautiful gift on Carrie's wedding day of my other son Vince and eight-year-old granddaughter Kayla. What joy these special loved ones have given me!

The little puppet-like ceramic caricature of a rose that Kayla bought for me with her own money when she was older (another little "sitty" thing— as she describes all my little knickknacks on display) is another precious gem.

The beautiful treasure box made of popsicle sticks with a coral on top and small sand dollars glued on the sides, signed by the artist himself, holds my stamps. This piece of art, handmade by grandson Albert (with the help of former daughter-in-law Holly) always warms my heart every time I pick it up and look at his XOXOXO on the bottom. No masterpiece is more precious to me than what this three-year-old's pudgy little hands created just for me!

So many things I would be heartbroken to part with. The paint-by-number velvet butterfly painting that Dad painted in his retirement years and Mom's framed embroidered flower garden hanging on the walls. The beautiful ceramic canister set Grandma Posey made for my wedding present. The rusty tin cup with the "cowboy motif" that was part of a set that Mom bought with green stamps at the grocery store—the set the family took when camping out. The little ceramic teapot that Mom gave me for my first home after my divorce that has "Home Sweet Home" printed on it.

Gifts from my sisters Judy and Bev—a snow globe/music box that plays *Amazing Grace* and the little plastic unicorn flower that dances in the sunlight and says "Have A Magical Day" on the front remind me of my sisters' great big generous hearts. How they have rescued me—even driving miles and miles through blinding snow and ice, so many times when I was in my darkest hours. And all the fun, crazy and joyful times we've shared.

In looking back, I saw that I had been down and out many, many times and much worse than what I had experienced in the last year; but I always made it through. My wonderful family and friends have always come through for me—helping me stay afloat after every crisis.

So many beautiful memories poured through my mind, clearing out those gloom and doom thoughts; replacing them with joyful, heartwarming, healing thoughts. Filling my heart with feelings of pride and gratitude for every year of my life—a rich life full of loving family and friends.

 On April 14, 2012, 3:00 p.m. the weather reports predicted that the storms were going to miss us.

Now Carrie and I could wholeheartedly go for it and hop aboard the *Titanic* for a night of first-class luxury. Gloom and doom thoughts were gone, and I was feeling excited for what life had in store for me in the future—like an immigrant on my way to the Promised Land.

I had been reminded not only of the wonders, the joy, the beauty in my life; but also, of my great strength—a product of all the disasters I had survived in my lifetime.

On April 14, 2012, 5:30, p.m. Boarding time for thirty-one-year-old Miss Madeleine Newell, and her sister on White Star Line's steamship *Titanic* (Haysville Community Library).

On the main deck, our purser greeted us, one of a cast of sixteen actors playing the parts of *Titanic* passengers and crew. She checked our tickets and showed us to our table. Carrie and I introduced ourselves to the others at our table, and they introduced themselves, and we shared the bios of the passengers we impersonated that evening.

While we were waiting for our food to be served and in between each course, the actors were milling about the dining room (the first-floor events room of the Haysville Library) interacting with the other passengers. The actors were all dressed according to their status—first class in the latest fashions of 1912, the steerage class in well-worn ragged clothing in need of repair. On our floor, first-class actors entertained us, along with an occasional pickpocket who was bold enough to escape the basement before they caught and sent him back below deck.

As I enjoyed the Chicken Cordon Bleu, the entrée in the seven-course meal, I was also thinking of the people in steerage who were having Irish stew and biscuits, fresh fruit and pickles. Thinking that, I bet those "passengers in steerage" are much more comfortable in their soft, worn-out, loose-fitting clothes than these women who are wearing corsets so tight they can barely breathe and the men wearing starched high collar white shirts.

And I thought of how wonderful it was to be sharing this night with my loving and so much fun-to-be-with daughter. And how comfortable and soft my life had become through the years. So what if my clothes were all worn and out-of-date, they sure were comfy!

The gala was a huge success. We enjoyed every minute of being entertained by the actors portraying Molly Brown, Bruce Isman the shipbuilder, Arthur Barratt the cabin boy, Mary McClellan, purser, and other *Titanic* passengers one hundred years ago. I found out later that the passengers in steerage class were entertained by an Irish jig by Isabelle, Victoria, and other steerage lasses.

April 14, 2012, 8:30 p.m. The predictions were wrong.

When I dropped off Carrie at her house, her husband Vince came out to tell us that a mile-wide tornado was headed toward Wichita. The three of us piled into my car after Carrie changed clothes and headed to my home to change and get my backpack, then straight to my sister Judy's a few blocks away. She has a basement with plenty of room for family living close by.

As we were making our way to Judy's, there was only one thought going through my mind—keep us all safe, God. I also forgot the things I had gathered on my cruise down memory lane. The three of us, my sister's kids and grandkids, my other sister, my uncle and his wife—all huddled together under mattresses in the basement. The smallest and youngest on the inside with the older ones on the outside.

And as we heard the roar of the tornado and the sound of debris hitting the house like icicles being thrown, we were all thinking and praying one thing—God keep us safe from harm.

As we slowly drove through the streets close by to go back to our homes after the tornado, we prayed our homes were still there. Upon seeing all the destruction surrounding us everywhere, we prayed a thank you for our lives being saved, for having and getting to a safe place out of this terrifying storm.

When I saw my home untouched—a huge limb torn from my tree lying just inches from my next-door neighbor—I cried tears of joy and thanks for my humble home with electricity and running water. And added a special thank you to God for all the treasures that my home held inside.

The next morning, I took a walk around the mobile home park to view the wreckage of the titanic tornado that had passed just a half-block away from my home. I saw trees, limbs, and debris strewn about everywhere.

When I saw how the tornado had mangled a six-foot wide steel pipe gate enclosing the park's maintenance storage area—just a few blocks away from my home—I gasped and almost fell to my knees. A cry—sorrowful, yet ecstatic at the same time—came up and out from deep within me—a cry of gratefulness to be alive and mourning for the losses of so many others who weren't as lucky as I was.

The news was non-stop for weeks covering the destruction in Tornado Alley that night of April 14, 2012—84 tornadoes across Oklahoma, Kansas, Nebraska and Iowa (43 in Kansas). Properties of the rich, the poor, the powerful, the powerless—nothing in the tornados' paths was exempt from damage. But thanks to our National Weather Service's Storm Prediction Center no lives were lost in Kansas.

Seeing the consequences of that night in the light of the next day and in the light of the re-discovery of the wonderful life I had, I knew that God had been right there and listening all the time I was going through all those challenges that past year. The problem was I hadn't been in receiving mode. I had been so into my "poor pitiful me mode" that I wasn't seeing all the beauty in this perfectly imperfect life I have had. Through all the crashes in my life, I had survived and had become a more loving and compassionate person as a result.

So, I finally had the answer to the question, "What am I going to do with my life now, God?"

Instead of feeling sorry for myself and thinking I was a failure, I would remember that no matter how much money I have in the bank, no matter what kind of job I have or if I have none at all; it can all be gone in an instant. Like the passengers on the *Titanic* and the residents in the path of the tornados, and the sale of the company I worked for—there will always be forces out of my control changing the course of my life.

Through the *Amazing Grace* of God and with the help of my amazing family and friends, I would survive—like the Newell sisters, who were put on the lifeboat by their father, who went down with the ship. I would joyfully and lovingly survive while remembering and being grateful for all those who had helped me to have the rich, full, wonderful life I had then and have now.

I would keep on discovering and re-discovering treasures wherever I am, wherever I go, whatever life throws my way. And would keep on remembering what is truly of value in my life—my children, my grandchildren, all my family and friends and having faith in a loving God who is watching over us all.

My Favorite Christmas Tradition
Nancy Breth

At the Writing Craft class December meeting at the Downtown Senior Center, the program was about holidays. From the many writing prompts that our leader Starla Criser gave us to use for the monthly writing exercises, I chose to write about "My favorite holiday tradition is…."

One of my favorite holiday traditions is sending out Christmas cards—a tradition passed down from my mother. For my piece to share with our group, I read my annual Christmas letter for 2025.

Everyone there encouraged me to enter my Christmas letter in the anthology as an example of writing other than a poem or a short story. So here it is.

Christmas 2025

Dear Family & Friends,

Every Christmas I enjoy recalling and savoring Christmases past and how much we all appreciated the simple things in life. Christmases now seem to be so much about shopping, spending lots of money, and keeping up with all the latest in fashion and tech gadgets.

My parents and grandparents lived through the Great Depression—endured struggles my kids and grandkids and I can only imagine. Mom told of having a few potatoes to feed the six of them for the evening meal and having to go to work at Boeing right after graduating from high school to help with the family bills.

They didn't spend hours and hours shopping for something new. They spent hours and hours darning socks, patching holes in the knees of their pants, making "new" clothes from flour sacks or remaking hand-me-downs. Worked day and night just to put food on the table and keep a roof over their heads. Never had much left over to buy gifts. But they were so thankful for the gifts they did receive (if any) at Christmas.

I am filled with sadness for the passing of this generation; this generation that knew how to make a little go a long way and who also taught us the value of the simple things in life. And I am filled with this full rich feeling of having been blessed with so very much love—a love I took for granted so much of the time.

When looking back at Christmases as a child, I remember only joy—the get-togethers with the grandparents, aunts and uncles, and numerous cousins. The joy of coming together, celebrating LIFE—good food, good company and lots of laughter. No one had much money; but boy did we have fun!

I don't remember many of the gifts I received; most of the gifts were clothes or things we needed. But always if there was something that we really, really wanted—like the bride doll I remember getting, it miraculously showed up under the tree. We never felt like our gifts weren't good enough.

One gift I remember most was a pack of Juicy Fruit gum my Uncle Jerry gave me one Christmas—wrapped and wrapped and wrapped in newspaper in a two-foot square box—and the laughter we all shared while I was unwrapping his "big" present.

I am so thankful for being taught the value of hard work, learning how to be self- sufficient like they were, and most of all for learning to appreciate and enjoy everything we had, each and every thing we were given.

And I am so thankful for all the great memories Christmases past that Mom and Dad and our grandparents made happen. We kids helping Mom make her fruitcakes, fudge, and peanut brittle. Cutting out and decorating sugar cookies; staining our mouths green and red from licking the bowl clean. Throwing tinsel at each other while decorating the tree, singing carols and making handmade gifts for Mom and Dad at school, and the fun family get-togethers.

The Christmases that my sisters and brothers and I made happen for our kids and grandkids when they were children were pretty much the same—filled with those priceless memories that can't be ordered from Amazon—lots of fun times filled with laughter. Yummy (and sometimes messy) food made with loving hands and watching the kids and grandkids squeal with delight unwrapping Santa's gifts. And best of all—getting together with family to share the Christmas joy.

Christmases are pretty quiet for my brothers and sisters and me now that we are the elders. Which has its own blessings.

Now, I enjoy getting together with family at Christmas time; and very much enjoy the quiet after the celebrations. Mornings and evenings in my flannel pj's with the loose elastic waistband, sipping tea while reviewing Christmases current and past with a big happy grin on my face. Thinking of all these lives that have filled my life with love and joy overflowing. And all the love and joy I have made happen for my kids and grandkids and other family and friends. And saying out loud, "Thank you, God, for this wonderful life you gave me. Thank you, thank you, thank you. Amen."

My dear family and friends, I wish *this* for you for Christmas and every day—the joy of coming together with family and friends, celebrating LIFE—good food, good company and lots of laughter. And that you too know this peace and comfort and joy of a life full of love overflowing.

But I Can't Do Anything!
Ruby Tobey

Many people think that if they don't draw or paint, they have no talent. But there are so many other skills that are more important and helpful to share.

For example, my friend Shannon grows beautiful flowers, especially Iris. And she shares the beauty of her yard to bring colorful joy to others.

And Terry does drawings and writes stories of her family history that she shares with me. Her husband, Don, uses his woodworking talent to teach young boys.

Sandy was a sweet friend who brought comfort to me with her caring heart and listening ear—especially in the months after my husband died.

And another is a wonderful cook who has not only provided for other's needs but shared her knowledge in a cooking class for girls.

I'm sure you have had a call or card from someone just when you needed it. Being friendly and letting others know they matter is one of the most important things, and some people have a natural talent for that.

I used the poem below when I wrote my Scribbles and Sketches book, and I'm using it again as a reminder that everyone is special in their own way. So, where you are a quiet encourager or someone whose talent gets noticed, you matter.

Talent
Ruby Tobey

You think you've no talent, nothing you can do,
but I know you better. I know it's not true.
Your talent may be simple, like cleaning or sewing,
not painting or writing but maybe just knowing
how to be friendly and just what to do
to put someone at ease and encourage them too.
Your talent's valued by God. It's needed here now.
He'll help you use it. He'll show you how.
You may never win praise in the eyes of man,
but you have a place in the Master's plan.

Whatever. Your hand finds to do, do it with all your might.
Ecclesiastes 9:10

Sculptured By God

Donald C. Septer

Out all across this great land
I can view the mighty works
Of God's strong hand
From the mountains high
To the valleys low
All is a treat for the eyes
And I am not left with any doubt
That this land was sculptured by God

For He left nothing out
From the bluest sunburst sky
To the darkest moonlit night
I can testify,
That God's hand
Has been at work
To shape this beautiful land

But most of all
What I enjoy the best
Is what I hear
When your heart calls
For God has sculptured
Both of our hearts
To fit together
To make one love in part

This has always been
Part of His plan
From the beginning to the end
Now as I look at you
I see love
In a heart that's true

So with the rising up of the sun
Each and every morning
We can enjoy His good work done
Because this love we now share
Was sculptured by God
As an answer to my prayer

Inspiration: The inspiration for this poem is my second wife, Belita. I wrote this poem for her. Each day I spent with her made me want to be with her even more.

Goodwill Hunting

Nancy Breth

"You discover treasures where others see nothing unusual," reads my fortune pulled from a cookie many years ago. I have it taped to the foot of my computer monitor. When my mojo is working, this is who I am—an adventurer out to uncover treasures right here, right now in the everyday seemingly ordinary days of our lives. Sharing these treasures is why I write. Hoping to light up another heart the same way mine feels when seeing the world with a joyful heart.

On this day in March, I needed a really big mojo boost. Was feeling as gray as my hair and also as flat. I decided I needed some color in my life. A few new colorful spring clothes seemed to be just the right fix for my shrunken mojo.

I remembered what Starla told us at our Writer's Group March meeting. A good way to get ideas for writing is to simply look around wherever you are, listen to people at a restaurant or walking around in a crowd; just observe. So, with that thought in mind and the thought of new clothes, I headed to the Derby Goodwill Store.

Seeing all those clothes to look through (clothes I could actually afford) lightened my heart right away. I grabbed the cart and marched right up to the Women's Short Sleeve Blouses rack to begin the hunt.
Shopping is not one of my favorite things to do; but that day my intention was to just enjoy observing the people and maybe also find a few new items to spruce up my wardrobe.

I began thinking of spring coming and how nice it would be to shed the winter coats and feel the sun warming my body. And maybe a road trip soon would heal the doldrums. And how nice it would be to open the windows of my apartment and let the clean, crisp air freshen up the place. And....

A shriek of joy reminded me of my intention for the day: Be here now; observe! I saw the source—a little blonde girl with long, wavy hair. She was with a man who must have been her grandpa. I tried to see what the excitement was about without staring. But all I could see was this tiny girl holding hands with this way older man, looking up at him as if he were Santa. Ahh! How sweet to be so excited by the simple things in life.

That jogged my memory of a Christmas when I was maybe ten years old. My Grandpa Miller dressed up like Santa and came to our house with our Christmas presents that year. My oldest brother and I knew it was our grandfather; but for the sake of our younger brother and two sisters and all the younger cousins that were there, we pretended to believe. We didn't have to pretend to be excited though—it was such a delight watching our seemingly gruff grandad playing Santa. And also—getting our gifts early (Christmas Eve) was such a special treat.

I thought my kids would love to hear stories of Christmases in my childhood days. How no one back then that we knew—family or friends at school—had much money or stuff. We never thought that we were missing out on anything. We were all very thrifty back then; nothing went to waste. That's why I love thrift shops and garage sales so much—recycling treasures.

Back to the hunt! A lady had joined me at the Women's Short Sleeve Blouses rack. Time to be alert for the "Goodwill Shuffle." (One person comes down one end of the clothes rack, the other person down the other end and when they meet, one shuffles around the other, noting where they left off, so they can continue down the rack looking through each item.)

The lady held her phone to her ear while searching through the short-sleeve blouses in our size. Oblivious to me or anything in her peripheral vision, she was engrossed in her multitasking—saying "uh huh" and "oh yeah" at regular intervals. (Kinda like I do with a few neighbors here in my senior apartment complex). She was definitely on a mission!

I moved to another rack of blouses, and soon a mom holding a small baby was scanning the rack I just left. She was also carrying a large bag that I assumed was full of diapers, bottles, and all that "stuff" a parent needs when taking an outing with an infant. Next, I saw a toddler playing hide and seek in a rack close by. When I started walking toward the tiny rebel, thinking I needed to "help" the mom, the toddler ran straight to Mom. My "rescuing" might have caused an uproar. So, I was glad the toddler ran to Mom and not for a rack of clothes farther away.

I almost gave up on my intention to just observe and enjoy when a little rosy-cheeked boy rushing to keep up with his mom, while also playing with a toy he wanted to buy, almost plowed into me. Instead of grouching, I smiled, remembering what a chore it was to lug my two little ones with me when shopping. My two were a year and eleven days apart—a lot like twins except in different phases of growth.

I was really getting into this, observing and enjoying as I continued scouring the blouse racks and then the pants. Doing the "Goodwill Shuffle" with the serious shoppers. Imagining who would wear that crazy loud fruity orange XL blouse or the size 0 shorts that would just barely cover their private parts. Imagining what my dad would have said and done if he had caught me in those shorts when I was 16.

Now there's a story in itself—how Dad and I butted heads so many times in my growing-up years and how I found out later as I matured how gentle and loving he really was.
I observed while trying not to get caught, a young woman skimming through the racks like a bug skimming the water, flitting all over the place. Her hair was in two topknots, eyes covered with huge glasses, dressed in mismatched clothes, I would not have the guts to wear outside a dressing room. But she had this bold attitude that said, "I am my own person and proud of who I am and how I look."

I tried to imagine what my life would have been like if I had had that kind of self-confidence, instead of being this mild-mannered, quiet, not-wanting-to-be-noticed person I have always been. But decided I am very much okay with being the quiet one.

The whole time, shopping and observing, I was also listening to the music playing in the background. Thinking about how uncreative the songs were, repeating the same phrases over and over and over. Wondering why those songs are so popular. Is it because we can easily sing along? I was about to diss the songs I was hearing and then the song "Louie, Louie" crossed my mind. Wondering how many times I heard and sang along to the lyrics "Louie, Louie, oh baby we gotta go" in the sixties and seventies. And also at Senior Center events in more recent years.

It was a busy day—I had to stand in line quite a while to get checked out that day. But I've found most Goodwill shoppers to be very patient and polite. Maybe it's because most of us are there because we can't afford the high cost of brand-new clothing and other items. We are quite content to hunt for our treasures and highly pleased when we find exactly what we are looking for and it also has a double discount tag on it.

I was in awe of the polite, cheerful and very helpful clerks that were checking out the customers. So rare these days where everyone is in a hurry, racing through life as if headed for a fire that needs to be put out. The clerks' attitudes seemed to calm the herd of people lined up waiting to be checked out.

I saw a guy sitting on a sofa close by while I was standing in line who didn't look too patient. Looked as if he had been waiting for hours. With a smile on my face, I asked him if he was having fun yet. He smiled back, showing me his dimples and his true nature of kindness and caring as he looked in my eyes.

The couple waiting in line in front of me appeared to be newlyweds or newly moving-in-togethers. They had their cart full of household items. I was admiring the guy's fox-red bushy hair and beard until the two looked each other in the eye and kissed as if they were the only ones in the whole building. I then blushed and turned away to look at baby clothes on a rack close by.

The kissing and the onesies reminded me of how sweet it was to be a newlywed—as if we were the only ones in the whole wide world and our love would last forever. And how soothing the smell of my freshly bathed and powdered babies was and how wonderful it felt to hold them in my arms as they drifted off to sleep. Ahh! The dreams we had back then. So different from how life turned out—that's a whole lot of stories to write for my kids.

By the time I reached the customer checkout counter, I felt a peaceful glow inside. Remembering so many treasured memories, I started feeling as colorful as the fruity orange XL blouse I had seen at the end of a clothes rack. Not only did I find some brightness for my wardrobe, but I also discovered my spirit of adventure was still very much alive and well inside this old body and mind.

I was feeling so at peace and full of goodwill as I was walking to my car that I just smiled when a drive-by texter almost ran me down. What I really wanted to do was trip him and watch as he threw his cell phone in the air and landed flat on his face. But that's a story that will have to be fiction, and what a great story that could be!

Goodwill hunting saved my mojo, and feeling my goodwill saved me from getting sued. *Quite a bargain for $15.00!*

Vacations
E. L. Morrow

Most family trips were to family members. Riding in the car was fun. Sometimes we would stop and eat at a restaurant. We always took the trip in one long day. Daddy did all the driving. He would load us into the car around 2:00 a.m. and drive until 9:00, then stop for food, gas, etc. We would then drive the rest of the day, usually arriving at some relative's a little before suppertime.

Once there, the adults would sit around and talk about people and events that happened when they were younger, or about people they used to know who were dead, sick, or in jail.

The kids were bored into semi-consciousness, as we knew none of those people or events. Since my sister and I were usually the only kids, we didn't look forward to what Daddy called "vacation." We had four cousins. If we visited one of them, we would sit in their rooms while they told us about all their friends, activities, or the various toys, stuffed animals, and pictures in their rooms. Occasionally, we would get to "go outside" and kick rocks, sticks, chase bugs, or notice fences containing various farm animals. Occasionally, we would walk around the area and be shown the house where "the meanest man (or woman) in the county lived."

As you can tell, family vacations were not a lot of fun for me or my sister. Fortunately, my father would periodically become mad at one or another of his siblings, and we would, as my mother said, "Go somewhere interesting."

One of those interesting trips was to Washington, D.C. My father was not a great museum person, but my mother thought it was a great way "to learn things that are not in books." I was probably ten years of age, and my sister was almost six. We went to the Smithsonian, and I saw dinosaurs. I don't remember T-Rex, but I was especially impressed with the Brontosaurus. Wow, it was big, and I was small. There were other prehistoric creatures on display—the Triceratops, and the huge bird with each wingspan bigger than our car. We saw the Washington Monument (big) and the Lincoln Memorial (also big). I concluded that everything was bigger in the past.

Another year when Daddy was on the outs with his family, we went to the Cherokee Reservation. We stayed in a cabin with a creek running a few yards from the back window. It was not air-conditioned, so the window was open. I had a strange need to get up and go to the bathroom several times during the night.

Both my parents loved the mountains. Well, we lived in Florida, where the highest spot in the state is just over 300 feet above sea level. When we reached a mile high driving through the Blue Ridge Mountains, I thought we were almost in heaven.

When my children were similar ages, I repeated the trip to Washington. Lincoln was still big, the Smithsonian was still awesome, and I was sure every person on the planet had decided to come to DC the same day we did.

In more recent years, I have had two trips that I remember with fondness. One to Butchart Gardens, which makes our Botanica look like a postage-stamp garden by comparison. The other was a day in the Sequoia National Forest.

I don't believe that bigger is necessarily better, but in these cases, bigger helps remind us of our place in the total scheme of things. We people with all our smarts, need to be reminded how vast and beautiful the world is—with or without our help.

Vacations are times carved out of the routine of work, deadlines, meeting others' expectations (or failing to), and daily responsibilities. When you retire, every day is a vacation. An opportunity to remember how big, beautiful, and overwhelming our world is. Retirement also allows us to do something good for someone else, just because we can, and it's the right thing to do.

Inspiration: Written as part of a writing exercise about memorable family vacations.

Of Course I Don't Have a Shoe Obsession
Ruby Tobey

I don't think I have a shoe obsession, but there are at least 30 pairs of dress shoes, sneakers, and boots in my closet. When I went to put away the summer sandals and light shoes and bring out the heavier winter ones, I found some I didn't remember having.

About $25 is my top price that I've paid for new shoes. But I am also a thrift store shopper, so most of my shoes cost $3 to $5 a pair, even my Skechers.

Thinking back, I wonder if my shoe collecting results from a childhood experience. It was sometime near the end of World War II when everything had been rationed, but they were getting better. I come from a family of seven and have two older sisters. Getting something new was a luxury. But I was going to get a new pair of shoes, and I was excited. Some of my other friends had pretty brown and white saddle oxford shoes. I pictured coming home with something like that. But the reality was that I ended up with solid brown lace-up shoes I thought were really ugly.

The small-town store that my folks could afford to take me to didn't have much choice of stock. So, I got practical instead of pretty as I had dreamed.

A couple of years ago I was in a Salvation Army thrift store, and they had a free room—things that hadn't sold that you could take. There sat a pair of pretty dark shoes with jewels on the toes, and they were like new and just my size. It must have been payback time for what I'd missed, and I love them. I feel like a happy child again when I wear them.

Afterglow
Donald C. Septer

Exchanging kisses
In the dimming glow of a setting sun
I find them sweet and tender
For my heart is surrounded
By moonlight and music
As I hold you close to me
In the soft light of the moon
I listen for the words
Your eyes are speaking to my heart
I listen intently to them
Closer, even closer now
My heart hears the promise of your love

As I close my own eyes
I breathe deeply
Inhaling the essence of your smile
For the radiance of it
Dazzles my weary eyes
There in the dark of night
I tenderly pull you close
To feel the beating of your heart
And the softness of your breath on my neck
Not only do I need to show you
How much I love you
But I want to enjoy you
And that promise of love

Suddenly a chill bolts through me
But it's not the wind
But the warmth of your love
That is driving away the coldness
Of the loveless world
That I had been forced to live in

Something inside lets me know
That as long as I hold you close
The promise I saw in your eyes
Will be kept by your heart
As the morning light
Breaks through the mist reflection
I yield my love to you, for yours
Now as I hold you close to me
I will be able to bask
In the afterglow of your love

Inspiration: This poem I wrote for my second wife as we were beginning to date. Seven months after I wrote this we were married.

That's What Trash Cans Are For
Ruby Tobey

One thing that makes me really angry is finding used disposable diapers that have not been disposed of properly. People leave them on the beach at the lake, in the grass at the park, and it's not unusual to find them in a parking lot.

Once we were riding our bicycles through the parking lot of our neighborhood park. What a mess! Disposable diapers that had been rained on and then run over by cars.

Modern parents, you have it so easy with disposable diapers and baby wipes. When my oldest sister had her first baby, I went to help her. They lived down a long country lane in a house with no electricity. Rural electrification was still coming to some counties in the 1950s. The way we took care of the diapers was to put them in a big pot on the stove and boil them. Then we took them outside to the hand pump and rinsed them before wringing them by hand and hanging them on the clothesline.

Disposables were not here yet when I had my three, but I had it a little easier. With the first two, I had a wringer washer. You had to fill the washer tub with hot water and let them wash a while, then put them through the wringer again into another tub of water for a second rinse, then through the wringer again before hanging them out to dry. I finally had an automatic washer by the time the third baby came along.

So, after all those experiences, when I see diapers that someone couldn't even bother to put in the trash, I want to arrest them. I would sentence them to at least six months of hand washing cloth baby diapers.

Where Were You on 9/11?

Joan E. Morrison

Well, short version. I worked for the government on the Air Force base. I was at a contract hotel off base inspecting when the first plane hit a tower. But we didn't see it on a TV. The front desk clerk at that hotel told us, but even she hadn't actually seen it on a TV.

By the time the second tower was hit, I was at the Marriott. My team and I had just walked in, and folks were watching on the lobby TV.

We stopped long enough to get the gist of things. It was horrifying but then my team's cell phones and beepers were ringing/going off—calling back to base.

They left while I waited for our hotel rep to come out. Working in a hotel myself, I knew processes were about to shift at the hotel. Instead of checking people out they would be busy canceling reservations, extending those already not checked out, waiting on the folks who had checked out and were at the airport to return and re-check in—all planes grounded— and dealing with everything else in-between.

The sales rep finally came out and confirmed this/can't inspect. Obviously, inspections lined up for that day were canceled. At that point, I also headed back to base.

Long line of cars to get in—unusual for that time of day—as I confirmed (later) a lot of military folks were being called in. None of us knew the extent of what was going on until we got back to base and could catch up via briefings and TV news. None of my team nor myself were particularly shocked in the moment as we were focused on what was going on around us—stunned but by the time any sort of realization set in we were back to base. As events unfolded that day, the horror of it all set in for me.

Note: This is the account of Susan Morgan, daughter of Joan Morrison.

Where Were You on September 11, 2001?

Joan E. Morrison

I was at home in Columbus, Ohio, waiting to go to work—watching the clock, with the television on in the morning, sometime after 8:30. I had to be there at 10, should I go in early to deliver "meals on wheels" for the Franklin County agency I worked for. As I watched a plane came on the screen headed for one of the towers—one of the twin towers in New York City.

In shock, I watched the whole thing: plane striking tower, its buckling, people falling out, everything. Then a second plane hit the second tower, same destruction. Then the fire department, the firefighters coming in. then news about another plane that struck the Pentagon. Then the news about another plane in Pennsylvania. Overtaken by hijackers, but those men were overcome by a couple of passengers, who prevented flying on to who knows where, but couldn't fly the plane. So, they steered into the ground, crashing. And in the meantime, other passengers calling home to say goodbye.

Well, after 10:00 a.m. I went to work. Other employees were kind of dazed. "What's going on here? Will there be more planes?" But there wasn't.

Curious about what happened, I have done much reading on the subject. Part of my research involved reading the book *Longitudes & Attitudes* by Thomas L. Friedman, a columnist and reporter for *The New York Times*. He was sent to investigate the story behind this attack on America. He claimed that "…the events of September 11th did not happen in a vacuum. They happened in the context of a new international system—a system that cannot explain everything but can explain and connect more things in more places on more days than anything else. That new international system is called globalization."
Through his explanations and my own understanding, I have become more aware of the complicated balances of nation-states, global markets, and individuals. Added into the complications of that are the web and the use

of transferring money or obtaining weapons that normally would be controlled by states.

I studied the map—countries in Asia and Africa were most involved when the attacks on 9/11 occurred: Syria, Iraq, Iran, Afghanistan, Pakistan, Saudi Arabia. As I sit with my maps, I am trying to learn about countries in Asia, Africa and Europe. I am amazed and thankful for my life here in America—the United States. Why haven't I found out much about all the other? Well, some "over there" hadn't tried to kill me and commit suicide in order to do it.

Self-Inspection Reflection
Donald C. Septer

I woke up to the sound of the alarm today
It seems like it's always been that way
I get up without thinking about
How this day is going to turn out

I've become complacent and have taken much for granted
And those things I didn't have I often ranted
It was then I realized the spirit of unthankfulness was upon me
And I decided then, this is not the way I want my life to be

I thought about all I had and had not given it one thought
All it seemed is I only cared about the things I sought
Keeping up with the world was all that I wanted
And never took notice of my blessing for those I shunted

Even late at night and when it was time to sleep
I expected the Lord my soul to keep
Never grateful for all the blessings that I had
And today for the first time I realized why I was sad

It came to me that I had disregarded the little things
And forgot about the things that happiness brings
So I took a deep breath and took my pen in hand
To take a look at where today I stand

I began to list the little things I've overlooked
The longer my list grew the more I shook
I began to see myself in an entirely different light
You see my ungratefulness gave me a terrible fright

To correct this wrong I got down on my knees
And began to pray, knowing God would hear my pleas

I thank Him for all His blessings those big and small
I didn't want to miss one or anything at all

I'm thankful for my family and for the sun above
And for Jesus's sacrifice that he gave us out of love
I remembered everything like my job and the sky
For my salvation because He was willing to die

I continued to give thanks for everything I could think of
And I didn't forget to thank God above for His Love
For He has watched over me since the day of my birth
To lead me and guide me during my time here on earth

Inspiration: Every once in a while we all need to do some self-reflecting. I wrote this as a self-inspection reflection of where I saw myself at the time.

IMAGINING

Happy Face
C. Holden

Put on your happy face, it gives you style and grace

anywhere or any place.

So put on your happy face.

When the storm clouds are a loom

and the weather is a gloom,

you can always put on a happy face.

When you are blue and feeling alone and don't know what to do,

just pick up the pace

and put on a happy and smiling face.

The Coolest Kid
Melinda Brooks

It's hard being the coolest kid in the seventh grade. Even when you have impeccable fashion sense and a rapier wit, society demanded total obedience to elders who had no interest in maintaining your social status. So, as Joe stood looking at the travesty that was once the site of the world's most perfect Beatle cut, he grieved and wondered what John and the boys would think.

Even though he was angry, he couldn't really manage to get steamed up at Granny. After all, she was old and not used to handling electrical implements. And she had been so proud of the electric haircutters she had just bought. It wasn't her fault she couldn't see well and had shaky hands. She meant well and had no idea of the damage she could inflict on his reputation.

Still, he hadn't really wanted a haircut. As a matter of fact, his sleek red locks made Melody (the coolest girl in seventh grade, also a fashion Maven) cling to his side like Delilah to Samson. There was no "I'd rather be dead than red on the head" for this guy.

Joe was not one of those boys who were easily corralled, and it took Granny awhile to get him to sit in the chair. She wrapped him in one of those fancy towels she got out of the laundry soap box, then pulled her brand new shears from the package. These weren't any old haircutters; they were the fancy ones with the built-in vacuum to make sure you didn't get any clippings on the floor while you cut each and every hair to the perfect length. No more bowls and pinking shears for this family.

When she plugged it into the wall, she got a big old smile on her face. "Well, Sir, how do you want it?" She grinned.
"Granny, just take a little off the ends, and please be careful," he replied.

She fumbled with the switch and finally handed it to Joe so he could turn it on. And when he did, the buzz of the clippers and the whir of the vacuum blended into a howl that nearly chased him from the room. But she was a supporter of American Industrial Ingenuity, and she would not be denied the opportunity to see her boy's hair properly coiffed by scientific progress.

It took a minute before Granny set to work. Joe imagined she worried the TV ads made things look easier than real life would prove, but maybe she was simply savoring a moment that she knew would stamp her name in the rolls of family history forever.

In a single pass straight back on the top of Joe's head, she took every hair down to the polished scalp. She couldn't have done better if she had been an Apache Warrior like the ones in the picture shows. Joe loved his granny.

The next morning, while standing in front of the mirror trying to figure out how to cover up all that shiny white scalp, it became clear to him that the cat would not sit on his head all day. He thought of feigning illness, but Granny never let them stay home from school unless they could prove they were dying or it was Saturday. So, he came to grips with the fact that he was going to be the only bald kid in seventh grade.

The room went dead quiet when he walked into class.

Then Melody laughed and said, "Nice haircut."

A Screaming Eagle!
Don Boldea

"Why can't I stay on here at home?" It seems my parents think I need to create an exit plan for when I graduate from the teen era of my life into the young adult era of my life and leave home. Anyway, I think that was the wrong question for me to ask.

They began the chat with a procedural seven-step suggestion that was framed in a well-designed plan of action for me.

Step one: College is behind you now. Get a job as soon as possible and start saving the bulk of your earnings for your own apartment, your own car, your own health and car insurance, and your own food and clothes.

Step two: Act as if this process is like sitting on a prickly <u>cactus</u>. It's both an incentive and relief when it's complete.

Step three: Imagine yourself as a <u>pilot</u> plotting your course for flying through life. Your goals will then become very clear to you.

Step four: Now you must find a professional financial investment firm and develop a long term financial plan.

Step five: Marry a beautiful and loving woman, a person who will be your life's partner. Have 3.2 children, two cars, a dog and a cat and a large five <u>bedroom</u> home with a very large mortgage. Finally, you will begin diverting your surplus salary into investment dollars for your deserved and inevitable retirement.

Step seven: This was the last piece of Mom and Dad's guidance. Prepare yourself for you and your wonderful wife becoming empty nesters. You won't have to ask us about our plans because we have already planned our seventh and last step. We have a lot of experience in this area ask your two older brothers and sister.

Mom said, "You see, we'll cash out our entire holding of assets, down size our personal possessions and move in with you and your delightful wife. You won't even know we're there because we'll be traveling much of the time since we won't have any restrictive financial obligations.

Then the other shoe dropped. "Dad and I won't need many niceties. Of course you'll have to have your guest room updated for us. You know a little paint here and there, new curtains and new carpet. And yes, the off suite bathroom will need a marbled tiled walk-in shower with a relaxing rain shower head including a set of surround water sprayers and a hand held rinse shower head. One other thing, it would also be nice if we had one those up and down adjustable beds. You know like those hospital beds. Ours is worn out."

Then Mom continued to describe their dietary needs. "You know us; we don't eat much because our daily diet is simple and healthy."

Mom continued, "In the morning, we will have a glass of orange juice, a cup of decaf coffee with two old fashion doughnuts each for breakfast. Oh yeah, and our assortment of special vitamins.

"For lunch we'll have our favorite dish, a fresh green cut garden salad with balsamic vinegar dressing and a hot ham and cheese sandwich with Black Tea.

"Dinner is also easy. We'll have another green salad with chunky Blue Cheese salad dressing. Then, our favorite served right off the grill, a hot and juicy ribeye steak cooked medium with just a morsel of pink in the middle, not medium well or well done. We would also like crispy French fries. To prepare our palates for the next bite of the tasty steak, we'll have a glass of red wine from a good wine vintner preferably a Cabernet Sauvignon from California. It'll go perfectly with dinner. After dinner we must enjoy a Kahlua or Baileys and coffee.

"That's about all we have to offer, Son. Son, your eyes are tearing. Is it something Dad and I have said? We just wanted to prepare you for adulthood.

I held it as long as I could but I just had to interrupt this transitional liturgy. I yelled out, "I'm not sure that I'll ever come out of my room again!"

Hey Mister <u>Screaming Eagle</u>, it's just the facts of life. After a short pause Dad smiled. "Son, we're sorry, we're just pulling your chain. Sit down, have a cup of coffee and <u>doughnut</u>. We love you, Son, but you are about to step into the next period of your life and whether or not you realize you have entered manhood or whatever you kids want to call it these days. But what we have mentioned above has now become your life's choices to make. Here, have another cup of coffee and a doughnut."

With fast thinking my immediate reply was, "But can I at least stay at home until I find that moment in time when I'm ready for the change over into manhood? You know I'm a little slow at thinking things through." Disappointment fell over their faces as did their smiles. Instead I smiled and said, "Gotcha!"

Inspiration: This was written as part of a writing exercise using the words cactus, pilot, bedroom, doughnut, *and* screaming eagle.

Just Singing a Song
Don Boldea

I love to <u>sing</u> love songs on and around Valentine's Day.

Hurtfully though because I've been told many times that my voice sounds like a <u>gopher</u> chewing on a slice of breaded and crisply French-fried <u>eggplant</u>.

My buddy likes playing <u>cupid</u> on Valentine's Day, especially between his sister and me. He says she's an embarrassment to him. It seems she made the girls basketball team and he didn't.

I turn <u>green</u> with envy each time I see her, she's so beautiful, but she doesn't see me as much more than a four eyed, tongue tied nerd who speaks Star Trek Klingon.

So, once again it's just another Valentine's Day that I celebrate by singing my repertoire of love songs to my pet Goldie the Goldfish. Yea, Goldie really doesn't like my singing either. She probably wishes she had fingers on her flippers so she can stick all them in her ears. In her fish bowl though she's a captive audience and has nowhere to run away or hide.

Although I believe she must enjoy my singing somewhat because she swims around and around in circles until she swims hard and fast into the inside glass of the fish bowl. She floats around on her back for a while and she does it all over again.

I just love to sing.

Inspiration: This was written as part of a writing exercise using the words cupid, eggplant, gopher, sing, *and* green.

What's a Dad to Do?
Starla Criser

"<u>Daaad</u>! Petey called me <u>chicken</u>!"

"Daaad! Abby called me…"

"Both of you! Stop it!" Trent yelled back, a headache growing stronger by the second.

He watched his *beloved* kids from near the playground. Maybe he could change his name from *Dad* to…

No, most of the time he loved being their father. But taking them to the park by himself for a picnic hadn't been his wisest choice. Their mother had warned him that it might be chaotic. He'd laughed away her premonition. He wasn't laughing now.

As he spread out a <u>black</u> tablecloth—actually a black trash bag he'd grabbed from the garage, he heard the distinct mocking sounds of "Quack, quack, quack!" Okay, his son apparently didn't know what sound a chicken made. But he wasn't going to correct him.

He pulled in a steadying breath and opened the picnic basket his wife had prepared for them. Peanut butter and jelly sandwiches in baggies. Cheese puffs, which would have his kids leaving yellow-gooey fingerprints on his car's leather seats. Perfect! And giant chocolate chip cookies.

Abby, his sassy four-year-old daughter, was suddenly at his side. Her sneaker-covered feet must have <u>whispered</u> as she came to him unnoticed. He held his breath for whatever outrageous thing she would say this time. "Daddy, we can't go swimming in the pool." Her big blue eyes glistened with tears and one dribbled down a pink cheek.

He'd promised them they could go swimming after they ate, and after they played a little longer on the playground equipment. "Why not?" He'd been sure it was open today.

Her lower lip trembled before she said, "Petey says there's <u>alligators</u> in the pool." She snuffled and wiped at another falling tear. "Daddy, I'm scared of alligators. I seen them on TV. They bites off legs and arms." She threw herself at him.

Trent squatted down and hugged her for a second. Then he lifted her up and turned to glower at his seven-year-old son by the swing set.

Petey took one look at his dad and hung his head. Slumping his shoulders, he walked slowly toward them. "I was only teasing, Abby. She should know better."

"She's four. You're her big brother," Trent said as patiently as he could manage. "She looks up to you. She trusts you."

Petey's eyes glimmered with tears as he looked at his sister. A sister now standing and grinning smugly. "I'm hungry," she declared and snatched up one of the sandwiches.

The stinker was quite an actress already. Heaven help them all in the future as she honed her acting skills.

Inspiration: This was written as part of a writing exercise using the words *dad, chicken, alligator, whisper,* and *black,* in combination with *writing about a picnic, kids and chaos.*

My Only Vice!
Connie Holt

I am as old as the hills, and as a teen,
I loved Coca Cola, and driving to school,
We'd stop at the station's pop machines,
Drop in a quarter, looking so cool.

As the fizz raced down our throats,
The cold refresher woke us up for class
The not too sweet taste made us gloat
Like heaven in a bottle of glass!

Then Coke's recipe was made anew,
Corn syrup made it way too sweet!
And it tasted like a vat of goo.

No coke treat for me for years-
I thought I would never taste the old
Coke of my long passed youth (tears)
Then I saw "A product of Mexico-"

On my grocery shelf, that sweet glass bottle,
They had never changed the recipe!
I grabbed a few, then to the checkout I toddled-
Then home to drink my long ago treat!

Love, Dad
Donald C. Septer

Robert was there when she was born and from that moment on, Carrie Jean was daddy's little girl. He played with her night and day, spending every minute he could with her. He knew that this was what he needed to do. He knew with the Vietnam War escalating he might soon be drafted. So, he wanted to make every minute of each day count. He spent as much time as he could with both his wife, Betty, and his little girl, Carrie Jean. He'd sometimes take off from work early when he could, just to have a little more time to be with them both.

Sundays were always special because when church service was over, weather permitting of course, he'd gather up his family and they'd go somewhere. Occasionally Robert would take his family out to Emerson Lake near Palmer and spend the day lazing around in the sun or splashing in the water. Sometimes they'd lie there on a blanket holding each other until the sun would go down. Betty would be on one side and daddy's little girl, Carrie Jean, on the other. He always kept an eye on the news to see how the war was going and prayed that it would be over soon.

Several years had passed and they were getting ready to celebrate Carrie Jean's third birthday. Robert had taken off from work early so he could be home for her birthday party. When he arrived at home, he found that his wife had been crying. When he questioned her about it, she told him they'd talk about it later.

After the party was over and things settled down. Betty went into the bedroom and came out with a letter and handed it to him. It was from the local draft board requesting that he appear for an induction physical in two weeks. The news felt as if he had been kicked in the gut. He sat there stunned by the letter, while she broke down and cried again. He got up and put his arms around her to comfort her. Although nothing he said or did would comfort her in her sadness.

The ensuing two weeks went by quickly. Robert notified his employer of his situation and was glad to know that they would hold his job open for him until he found out whether he passed his induction physical and was drafted or not. His coworkers gave him a farewell party of sorts, although he might return after his physical. They said they didn't want to take the chance in case he passed and was drafted. It was quite the sendoff for one of the company's best employees.

On Sunday evening of that week, he was scheduled to take the bus at 7:30 p.m. As had become their usual habit, the family went to church, and when it was over all the church members came and wished him well and every one of them promised to look after Betty and Carrie Jean while he was gone.

After leaving the church, they embarked on a farewell picnic. Robert had already packed his bags the night before, so he would be ready to go when they got back. The sun shone brightly across the lake making the water shimmer as if it were glass. It was quite warm for this time of year. Although it was early September it was beginning to cool off, but this day was exceptionally warm and made the day all that more enjoyable.

 After they ate, Robert took Carrie Jean over to the swings and pushed her. The higher he pushed, the more she laughed. She always got tickled when he pushed her on the swing. After five minutes she was tired, so they went back to the where Betty had been sitting on the blanket watching. He noticed her eyes were red, and that she had been crying, but he made no mention of it.

For the next few hours, Robert and Betty lay on the blanket next to Carrie Jean and held each other, closer than he ever remembered holding her. With such a lazy afternoon before them, it was not long before all three of them were fast asleep. He was the last to fall asleep as he wanted to cherish this moment with both in his arms.

Realizing that it was getting late, he loaded up the car, and the family drove home. His bus was due to leave in a few hours, and he wanted to shower and clean up before he left.

At the bus terminal, they stood there holding each other, tears cascading down Betty's cheeks. He did his best to try to "be brave" as he sniffed back every tear that he could. Finally, the bus driver called out the last call to board. He picked up Carrie Jean and gave her a big hug and a kiss goodbye from her daddy.

Slowly, Robert turned to Betty, and she fell into his arms sobbing uncontrollably. He gave her a gentle but firm kiss goodbye and promised her he'd write to her when he could. They both knew that he would pass his physical and be drafted. As the bus pulled away, he watched his two favorite girls wave goodbye, then just before the bus turned the corner, he saw Betty take Carrie Jean by the hand and start walking towards the car.

As expected, Robert passed the physical with flying colors, and they drafted him immediately. He was processed through the enlistment procedures. Filling out what seemed to be reams of forms, he thought he was going to get writer's cramp before he completed all of them. Afterwards, he and some other recruits were ushered into a large room where all the other draftees waited. All were asked to stand and to raise their right hands as they swore their allegiance to defend the nation against all enemies, foreign and domestic. Afterwards, the recruits were herded off to a cafeteria for a quick meal before they taken to the airport to be flown to their service's boot camp.

After surviving boot camp, they notified Robert that he would have the honor of going to Vietnam. He received a short leave and could go home and spend some time with his wife and daughter. It was strange being home after he had been through boot camp. Here he had a soft bed, a beautiful wife and his little girl to be with every day. He was happy being home where he could spend every hour of every day with his two favorite girls, Betty and Carrie Jean. But he knew this happiness would not last.

Three days before Robert was to leave for Vietnam, he had gone to bed early. After talking a bit with Betty, they both fell asleep. Sometime in the night he woke up from a dream. It upset him so that he had to get up and go into the living room and sit in the chair for a while. As he sat there, he played the dream over again in his mind.

In his dream, Robert was a pallbearer for a fallen soldier. There were many people there that he didn't recognize, so he was unsure as to whose funeral he was a partaker of. He noticed that the casket lid was open, so he tried to move closer to see if he could recognize the soldier. As he struggled to move closer, he heard a voice in the background bark out the command, "Ready." He was moving closer when the same voice issued a second command, "Aim."

Everything around him began to move in slow motion. He knew or sensed that they were giving this soldier a twenty-one-gun salute. Just as he looked into the casket, he heard, "Fire." As his eyes surveyed the soldier's face, he recognized it as the one he had seen in the mirror hundreds of times when he shaved. It was his. The gunshots echoed through him like an electrical shock, and it broke him out of his thoughts.

After he had sat there for what seemed like an hour thinking about his dream, he decided to give his little darling, Carrie Jean, something to remember him by if he got killed in Vietnam.

When he finished the letter, he wanted to hide it in some place where his wife Betty wouldn't find it and cause her undue stress and worry. He figured the best place to hide the letter would be in the wedding registry of their family Bible. He prayed that if he came back alive, then he would be able to destroy it. But if he didn't make it back, well, then Betty would eventually find it when she went to enter information about their daughter's wedding. He knew that if he were killed, his wife would be too grief-stricken to write about his death immediately in the registry of the family Bible. As time passed, she would be too busy raising their daughter Carrie to remember to do it then. So, he felt confident that his letter would be there on or about the day their daughter would get married.

Putting the Bible back on the shelf, Robert returned to bed and fell back asleep. After rising the next morning, he got up as if everything were normal. Betty had let him sleep in the last two mornings while he was home. Finally, the day arrived for him to leave. Saying goodbye this time was the hardest thing he believed he ever had to do, especially in view of his dream. His heart was in his throat the entire time. After waving goodbye for what he prayed would not be the last time, he boarded the plane, and he was Vietnam bound.

Robert's arrival in Vietnam was a shock to his system. It had been early winter, November, back home. With snow on the ground and temperatures hovering around twenty-five degrees in the "heat" of the day. In Vietnam, the temperatures were in the high nineties, and the humidity was so thick, he thought he could swim in it. He couldn't believe his luck when he learned he had drawn an assignment to the headquarters in Saigon.

After arriving there, he settled into a daily routine, pulling guard duty when he had to. Then it happened. He had that same dream again. He woke with a start and happened to notice the date, January 28, 1967. Since he couldn't go back to sleep, he got up and wrote a letter to Betty.

My dearest Betty,
How are you today? I'm fine. I couldn't sleep, so I decided to write you a letter. Not much has been happening around here. Charlie's agreed to call a truce during the Tet holiday. It'll be good to get some time off from the war. It's been rather hectic with the war going on twenty-four hours a day, seven days a week. It seems that every day I see troops coming from and going to the front. Those coming back look so haggard and most were completely worn out.

Those I watched going to the front have a fear in their eyes that can be seen a mile away. I pray each day that the good Lord will keep watch over me while I'm here and get me home safely so that I can spend the rest of my life with you and our little "Carrie Jean." When I'm feeling down, I take out the picture I have of the both of you I took on Carrie Jean's third birthday. I may not be home for her fourth birthday, but I know I will be there for the rest of them.

I am scheduled to be on guard duty tomorrow night on the eve of the Chinese New Year, which the Vietnamese call "Tet." They'll celebrate the evening before by having parties and lots of fireworks, much like the way we celebrate Independence Day. Since the cease-fire has been in effect, the morale of the people here in Saigon has lifted a great deal. With the war and all, I can understand their need to "let their hair down," so to speak. My buddy Jim and I have drawn guard duty tomorrow night, and it will be great knowing that there will be a friendly face out there that I can run into in the dark. Jim and I have this pact. We will watch each other's backs while on guard duty. Jim's been a good friend since I got here. We both arrived in Saigon on the same day. He had been "in country" for a couple of weeks before he was assigned to Saigon, where we met. Anyway, I don't want you to worry; I got somebody covering my back.

Well, honey, I have to close for now. I need to take a shower and then get this off in the mail today before I report for duty. I'm on duty from 7:30 a.m. to 4:30 p.m. and then I'm off until I report for guard duty at midnight. To avoid the boredom of doing guard duty, we only pull six-hour shifts, so I'll be off guard duty by 6 a.m. and I'll be in bed by 6:05 a.m. (ha ha). Oh yeah, I was checking the calendar yesterday, and I now have just a little less than eleven months to go before I'll be out of here and on my way back home. If all goes well, I should be home by Thanksgiving. They tell me it's bad luck to keep track of how long you have until you return to "the world" (that's what they call the United States here). I don't believe in that superstitious gobbledygook. I have faith in God for my safekeeping. Please pray for me as I pray for you and Carrie Jean.

Love always,
Robert

P.S. I almost forgot. I hope you both have received the Christmas present I sent you. I hope you get them before this letter reaches you. I'm sorry I was so late in getting them sent to you as the war has kept me busy and I just didn't have time to get them mailed any earlier than I did. See you when I get back home, love ya.

Betty was just laying down the letter she had received from her husband Robert when she heard the front doorbell ring. She had been in the kitchen, so she had to hurry into the living room to answer the door and see who would visit her early in the morning.

As she was walking towards the door, a feeling of dread shot through her like lightning, and she almost stopped in her tracks. Her hands began to shake as she reached for the doorknob. That moment will be forever etched in her mind. Standing at her front door were three officers, and the last thing she heard one of them say was, "Ma'am, we regret to inform you...."

Betty and her husband, Phillip, celebrated their daughter, Carrie Jean's eighteenth birthday. Being her eighteenth birthday, they gave their daughter the biggest party they could afford. Betty had remarried thirteen years ago. She needed a father for her daughter after losing her first husband in the Vietnam War. Carrie Jean was growing up and was missing her real father. At first, she rejected every advance of Phillip's friendship. Then, one day, the ice broke, and eventually over time they grew closer, although they never shared the closeness that a father and daughter share. At her birthday party, Carrie Jean surprised them both by announcing that she was getting married. Although they were surprised, they were still incredibly happy for her.

In the ensuing weeks, Betty and Carrie Jean began to prepare for her special day. The months went by until the night before her wedding day arrived. Carrie Jean and her mother had just returned home after the last rehearsal and rehearsal dinner. The two of them were sitting there talking and reminiscing about her growing up. Then Betty remembered something she wanted to do. She went to the bookcase and pulled out their old family Bible.

She had Carrie Jean sit down at the table so they could fill in the information about her wedding and her fiancé's family history. Thumbing through the Bible Betty found the wedding registry, and she was surprised to find a letter there. It was unopened with only the name, Carrie Jean, on it. Not thinking much about it, she handed it to her daughter. It had been so long that she failed to recognize the handwriting of her first husband.

Carrie Jean opened the letter, and as she began to read, she burst into tears. Dumbfounded by her reaction to the letter, Betty turned in her chair and asked, "What's the matter, Carrie? Why are you crying?"

Through her tears, Carrie mumbled that the letter was from her daddy. Betty was floored by this revelation. It was as if her first husband had reached across time to this day.

After calming Carrie Jean down, Betty asked, "Do you feel like reading the letter out loud so I can hear it, or do you want to see if it's personal and just read it yourself?"

"Mom," Carrie Jean said, "I think it would be best if we both shared it together." Carrie Jean steadied herself as she began to read the letter that was dated October 31, 1967.

Memories flooded to Betty's mind as she fought back tears. When Carrie Jean saw that her mother was crying, she asked her, "What's the matter? Why are you crying?"

"Carrie, that letter was written two days before your father left to go to Vietnam." She thought she saw something cross Carrie's face, but she wasn't sure, so she told her to read the letter. Carrie looked at her mother, then at the letter and began to read.

To my sweet Carrie Jean:

There is so much I want to say to you that I'm not sure where to begin. I imagine you are quite puzzled by this letter, but if you are reading it now, it means that I did not make it back home. So, I'll do my best to explain why I wrote it to you. As you know, people sometimes have premonitions about things, and tonight I had a dream that I was going to die in the war, and I couldn't comprehend not being with you as you grew up. So, this will be your father reaching out to you from the grave. I want you to know that I never told your mother because she was already fearful of my going to Vietnam.

I am struggling with writing this letter knowing that I may not get to watch you grow up. I'll miss taking you to school on the very first day you go; I'll miss all the birthdays that you'll have. In fact, I know I'll miss everything that makes one's life worth living. I love you and your mother more than life itself, and I pray to God every day that if it's His will that I'll be able to come back home alive and be able to destroy this letter before you or your mother discovers it.

Since you're reading this letter, I can't even imagine what you have gone through, with no father to be there when you needed him most. Right now, I'm sitting here trying to think of the right words to write down what I want to say, but it isn't easy. My heart feels like it's made of lead; it's so heavy. I want you to know that even in death, I still love you. God, I wish I didn't have to go, but I must. Let me explain why.

I've always tried to do what's right and live an honorable life so that it might be an example to others. I never had it in me to try and dodge the draft by leaving the country or going into hiding. That's a coward's way out, and that just isn't me. I don't think I could look at myself in the mirror every morning knowing that I had done such a dishonorable act as that, so I pray you'll forgive me for not taking the easy way out just so I could be with you right now. Your father loves you enough, that he'd rather die an honorable death than bring any shame on you that you might have to live with for the rest of your life. So, this is why I chose to go, but I go with hopes that I'll come back alive.

Since you're reading this letter, I didn't make it back to destroy it. It is my hope that your mother will have remarried. She's the finest woman I have ever known, and I wouldn't want her to live a life of loneliness because of me. She needs to be loved, and I hope she finds a good man who loves her as much as I do now. I pray that if she does remarry, he'll be a good father to you, and you will learn to love him as much as I love you and your mom.

I know your mother may be wondering about this letter, so I'll continue with my explanation. As you already know, after I had the premonition, I wrote this letter and had to find a hiding place where the letter would not be found for the year I'd be gone. After much thought, I hid it in our family Bible, because I thought it would be the last place your mother would look for something and discover the letter before my year was up. If I didn't make it back, I knew the Bible would probably stay on the shelf undisturbed until the day or close to the day you would be getting married. I figured with my death and her grief, followed by her having to raise you all alone, she wouldn't think about the Bible until you would be getting married. I knew she would want to write your wedding information in the Bible. So that is when I wanted you to discover this letter.

Anyway, it must be close to your wedding day for you to be reading this letter. I want you to know now that if it is in my power to be there for your special day, I'll be there. If I'm not, please know that I'll be watching down from Heaven and sharing this special day with you. Well, I'm gonna close now as it's getting late and I need some rest. Just remember this, if it happens to be raining on your wedding day, it won't be raindrops that are falling, but teardrops of my joy that are falling from Heaven to shower you with all my love.

It is my prayer that you will have a blessed life, filled with love, and I pray the only sorrow you ever suffer is not having me in your life. One more thing before I close. I will always remain close to you, wherever you may be and if you want to be close to me for any reason, remember me not with your memory but with your heart, and I'll be there.

Love, Dad

Haiku Things to Do in Physical Rehab
Connie Holt

Watch Sesame Street!
Brings back memories with kids,
And it makes you smile!

Then, get out paper.
Pen some of those. memories—
Voila! Journaling.

Watch some Deals and Steals,
But leave your credit card home—
You are just looking!

Watch some musicals.
Tap your toes with the Forties
Instant Energy!

Airport Lost and Found—
Looking for her dad's eyeball—
I hope it's not real!

Vehicle Drug Tests
At Border, they will be caught.
Great job, border guys!

In the afternoon,
Find a crazy fun movie,
And laugh your head off!
Say Yes to the Dress
Mother daughter dynamic
Not for everyone!

So Many Signs
Donald C. Septer

On the street the lonely man stands
Hoping passersbys will read the sign in his hands
A cry for help to his fellow man
Hoping they'll help him anyway they can

Traffic passes by and no one will stop
After a time, the sign slowly starts to drop
What's wrong with everyone can't they see
I'm willing to help them in return for free

Slowly a tear slides down his face
As he turns away from his waiting place
Walking off with his thoughts of despair
Wonder why no one really seems to care

As night falls upon the alley way
He stoops to crawl in the box at the end of day
In the glow of a candle, he closes his eyes to rest
Soon his head drops down upon his chest

Dreams of memories and memories of dreams
Rush into his sleep like many fast-moving streams
Flashing by so quickly in rapid succession
Leaving his heart tied up in depression

His body jerks in a frightful fright
As his dreams battle in the nightmarish night
Finally, he awakes in a cold sweat
Opening his eyes, he sees it's not morning yet

Sobbing, he lays back his head to rest
Silently waiting for the calm to return to his chest

On with Life: Memories and Imaginings

In the darken shadows he finds no sleep
Soon the pinkish glow of morning starts to creep
The growl inside tells him it wants to eat
As he struggles to climb upon his feet
Many a day he's gone hungry inside
Humankind had chosen that he be denied

Today luck has come his way
A kind soul gave him money to pay
Ravenously he eats as others look on
Judgmentally hoping he'll soon be gone

Today he thinks that today might be the day
That God will send that special someone his way
As he takes a moment and says a prayer to the heavens above
Then picks up his sign that reads "I need a hug, and I just need love"

Inspiration: As I was walking, the image of a man holding a sign came to mind. So, I took out my pad and pen and wrote this poem from that image.

Life can be 'A *walk in the Park*'

David Larimore

I hope you enjoy a walk in the Park this Spring,
To hear flowers bloom and hear the songbirds Sing.

Maybe enjoy a picnic with someone you love,
As you sit on a blanket, sunny blue skies above.

Springtime in the Park, you might enjoy some quiet,
But once schools out, the park scene is like a riot.

Kids of all ages screaming as they run,
It's hard to tell, are they hurt? Or having fun?

And watch out as balls and Frisbees are thrown,
With those wild throws there is NO Safe Zone.

And Moms screaming at kids to "PLAY NICE"
Yelling a warning, "Don't make me tell ya TWICE."

I'm just kidding about how much chaos is out there,
Depending on time of day, you MIGHT find peace anywhere.

Springtime quiet and Summer cale CAN be the same.
Because most kid are indoors, playing a video game.

My Favorite Place
E. L. Morrow

The access lane runs for about a mile off the main road. The private road has been recently "re-rocked." The new gravel is still loose, so progress is slow. Soon, I realize the only sound is the crunch of the auto tires against the granite stones.

The path ends abruptly, with just enough room to turn a car around. Tall grass surrounds the parking area on three sides. I am glad I remembered to wear a jacket and closed shoes. The five-and-a-half foot-tall grass has sharp edges, capable of slicing into the skin deeply enough to draw blood.

Even with my precautions, stepping through the grass still stung and discomforted my hands and fingers as I pushed the blades aside to enter. I knew the small pain would be worth it as it only took three steps before finding myself on the other side.

Farmers had been planting this jungle-like grass in a five-foot-wide band to discourage the uninitiated from finding the glorious beauty just beyond. They also cut the grass in the fall for animal feed during the colder months. But this being late April, everything, including the grasses, is at its peak.

I step out of the grass, and there it is. The first thing to hit me is the fragrance. Nearly two hundred different species of wildflowers live and bloom here each year. At any given time, fifty to seventy-five will be in bloom. So, the aroma greeting a visitor is never the same from one day to the next. As something new blooms, or the breezes shift to combine the scents in different concentrations.

Today, it's a light and sweet smell that welcomes me. Daisies, gladiolas, and gardenias combined with at least a dozen others, with no name—as far as I know.

The second thing a visitor notices is the warmth. The sun on my face and these scratched hands remind me it will soon be too hot for some of the wildflowers to bloom.

The third thing to be noticed is the beauty. A bouquet of color that words cannot describe. The bright reds, yellows, and blues catch my eye first. But after a few moments, the paler colors take center stage in the mind: pastel yellows, pinks, salmon, oranges, cream, and even some pale green blossoms. One also begins to notice the small, delicate blooms—some requiring a magnifying glass to view clearly.

It's a place of relaxation, a sanctuary for meditation, and a center for renewal. Once there, I don't want to leave, but the gnawing feeling in my tummy says it's time to go. But I can come back any time—because it exists at the center of my spirit.

I'm usually there alone, but sometimes I sense the presence of others, just out of sight. Once, I thought I heard my father calling my mother, "Rose, where are you?" I must be confused; they both died decades ago. Or perhaps not confused, only aware that all we have loved are still close.

Diamonds for a Dance
Donald C. Septer

From across the crowded dance hall floor
I saw you and wanted to get to know you more
There in the dim lights and shadow's cast
Stood the woman my true love at last

I drummed up the courage to ask you for a dance
But in my heart, I was hoping for a little romance
And as we moved slowly around the dance hall floor
I knew I wanted you then forever more

As I held you close tightly in my arms
I dreamed what it'd be like to taste your charms
We twirled and whirled until the music was through
I knew by then I was totally in love with you

Instead of letting you go I asked for a second dance
Didn't want to think that I might not get another chance
You looked at me and said, "Yes" and it set my heart on fire
I was hoping that when the dance was through you'd feel my desire

As I held you close, I didn't realize that the time had went so fast
And to my disappointment our dance came to an end at last
I looked at you and smiled and thanked you for the dance
I wanted to ask you out, but I was afraid you'd rebuff my advance

So, I spent the rest of the night trying to get another dance with you
I knew in my heart I wanted more and two just wouldn't due
So, every time the DJ would pick a new song to play
I'd get upon my feet, and I would head your way

But every time I did someone would always be there
Jealous as I was, I had to act like I didn't care

I had to do something if I was ever to get you to look my way
So down in my heart I came up with something clever to say
As the dance was coming to an end, I made my move
I was in love with you, and I had something to prove
I wanted you to know that being with me was where you belonged
So, I jumped at the chance as the DJ began to play the next song

I walked up to you and said, "I'll give you rubies for a kiss"
I knew it's something I didn't want to miss
And if you're looking for true romance
I'll give you diamonds for a dance

I could see a surprised look upon your face
So, I took the time to make my case
I told you that if you were looking for love
I could be that man with the love your thinking of

So, if you'll just consider what's in my heart
I can be your one true love right from the start
You stood up and took my hand, and we walked onto the floor
There in my arms as we dance you whispered, "tell me more."

Inspiration: I heard a phrase that I misunderstood from a song. Thought I had heard the phrase, "Diamonds for a Dance" but that wasn't what was said. But I liked the title and wrote the poem from it.

Found, Lost, Found and Lost Again
Don Boldea

Dad sent me to the neighborhood barbershop to get a haircut before the fast approaching first day of school before Labor Day. Dad gave me fifty cents for a twenty-five-cent haircut. The extra quarter was for the barber to give me a gentleman's styled cut, not just trimming my mullet!

Over the summer I had let my hair grow longer than my dad cared for me to, yet he let me do it anyway. By the middle of July my hair was nearly shoulder length. I caressed my beautiful locks every day with about a quart and a half of Rose hair oil. Finally, I fashioned my hair into a huge rolling pompadour with a finished coat of a brightly colored red sheen like on a new '67 Chevy, really cool, huh?

What's way cooler yet I was coming back from the barbershop with my mullet which had grown and soon to be groomed into an exciting Niagara Falls picture of flowing magnificence. Like the red Chevy, I was really cool; the style was yet to be copied by Billy Ray Cyrus.

Okay, back to the point. The barber's nickname was Smokey; I don't think anyone of his customers or neighbors knew his real first or last name. He was a fairly good-looking man in his mid-sixties and always wore the standard barber's frock. Smokey's nickname came about because he was almost always smoking a cigarette while cutting a man's hair. Finished, Smokey applied hair spray to keep the customer's nearly bald head of hair in place. The cigarette sometimes caused the flammable hair spray to ignite. This caused a bilious flame and singed the rest of a man's almost bald head to completely bald. "Oh shoot, sorry, no charge!"

While Smokey cut your hair, he talked constantly about his early life, his military service, his married life, even though he was now a widower. His only vice was a compulsion to stop occasionally, alright very often, and reach for a bottle of a reddish-black liquid called Geritol and take a swig. Geritol, supposedly a vitamin supplement, was an elixir whose base was alcohol. As you can imagine, the best time to get a good haircut was to be his first customer of the day. And he had only one haircut style, a modified WWII Marine haircut, high and tight.

On that fateful day, just as I reached the barbershop, resting there on the ground in the corner of the L-shaped strip mall was a dollar bill. I jumped on that bill like a duck on a June bug.

Next door to Smokey's Barbershop was Jenson's Sundry. Here the dollar would buy a hamburger, fries, a vanilla milkshake with a quarter dollar left over for five games on my favorite pinball arcade. Happy days are here again! I found manna from heaven.

At Jenson's Sundry you could fill a medical prescription, buy cosmetics and other toiletries, buy costume jewelry, camera film, newspapers and comic books, toys, a host of personal needs and a multitude of domestic supplies.

This neighborhood sundries store also included a lunch counter, three sit down booths, a Wurlitzer music machine, a pinball arcade, a pool table, a comic book stand and a small dance area. What a great hangout for everyone, young and old.

Okay, I thought more of my pleasures than the necessity of a haircut. I stuffed the dollar bill into my pocket and I went off to Jenson's Sundry. Mr. Jenson greeted me with his usual, "What's up, Jimmy?"
I blurted out, "Hello, Mr. Jenson! I'm here for your seventy-five-cent luncheon special. You know, your famous hamburger, fries, vanilla milkshake and with a quarter dollar left over to play at least five games on my favorite pinball machine."

With a big smile he replied, "Okay, young man, let's get you started."

The big meal was tasty. I played ten games on the Baseball arcade. I won a few free game plays because of my high game scores. Then, I suddenly remembered about the haircut. I hurried up to the cashier's counter, as Mr. Jenson called it, to pay for lunch and the pinball games.

Mr. Jenson said, "Well, Jimmy, I believe that'll be an even half dollar and that includes the tax."

Well, I reached deep into my front right pocket for the dollar bill. The only thing I pulled out was a Double Bubble bubblegum wrapper, with a Joe Palooka comic printed on the inside of the wrapper and pocket lent. I reached into my left front pocket. I didn't even pull out the fifty cents Dad gave for my haircut. My heart stopped temporarily. I've lost all of my money.

Mr. Jenson watched me. As I looked up at him, he saw the fear in my eyes. I stuttered ashamedly and said that I had lost the money and that I really did have a dollar and fifty cents. He looked at me and said with an understanding smile, "Jimmy, I'm sure you did have a dollar and fifty cents in your pocket. Perhaps you can ask your dad for an advance on your allowance?"

I was about to tell Mr. Jenson, no I can't do that when I caught a glimpse through the kitchen door. There was a mile-high stack of dirty dishes from the lunch crowd. Instead, I asked him timidly, "Couldn't I just work off what I owe you? I can wash dishes, sweep floors, dust shelves and hand out the handbills for your different weekend specials, how about it?"

Without hesitation, he said, "That's a good offer, young man. Yes, a good offer. You're on!"

After I washed the dishes, swept the floor, dusted the shelves and promised to come in Saturday morning to hand out the handbills for the sundry. It was now time to go home and face Dad.

Dad wasn't happy with my explanation but was happy with how I resolved my debt with Mr. Jenson. Now, how was I to deal with the monies Dad gave me for the haircut? I had to think about that.

As I readied for bed, I was taking off my jeans when I felt something stiff in my blue jean watch pocket. I reached into the pocket and pulled out the dollar bill wrapped around the two quarters. I had forgotten where I put the found dollar and haircut money.

Excitedly, I ran downstairs to explain to Dad what I found and how it happened. Calmly he looked at me and said sternly, "That's great, but you are still grounded for a week because you didn't go directly to the barber as I instructed. Now, go to your room and go to bed. You still have to get your haircut tomorrow! The mullet goes too, young man."

Redundant? Yes! I found, lost, found and lost again. That's just the way it goes sometimes in a young man's life.

The Lonesome Old Man
Donald C. Septer

Rocky had thought that he and his girlfriend had a good thing going, but today they got into an argument. What started as a simple misunderstanding turned into a fight. In a fit of anger, he stormed out of the house to take a walk to cool off before returning. He was thinking maybe it would be best to break off their relationship as he saw the problem was all hers.

While he stormed about, he ended up down at the river. Rocky began to walk along its banks to ease his frustration. He knew that walking there always brought peace to his spirit and gave his soul a much-needed rest. What helped him most was the solitude of its surroundings. This was his place to get his head together.

As Rocky drew near the bridge, he noticed a solitary figure standing about halfway across. The figure was staring down at the river below. Still angry, he wanted to ignore the man and walk on by. But as he approached him, something about the man attracted him. He felt a desire to stop and speak to the man. Between his anger and the desire, he struggled with the urge to engage him in conversation. It was if he couldn't control himself. Before he knew what happened, he heard himself say, "Hello."

The sound of Rocky's voice made the man jump as if he had been lost in his thoughts. "I'm sorry, sir," he said. "I didn't mean to startle you."

The man slowly turned toward him and stared at Rocky for a few moments. He could see light but distinct tear tracks that had fallen from the man's eyes. Pretending not to notice, he asked, "Are you alright, sir? Is there anything I can do for you?"

With a slight smirk on his face 968 the man said, "If you can move back the hands of time and let me live my life over, then you can help me."

Somewhat shocked by his answer, Rocky was tongue-tied for a proper response. The man grinned then turned back to staring at the river. At a loss for words, Rocky stood there, then mumbled something totally unintelligible.

"Did you say something to me, son?" asked the man.

Embarrassed, Rocky replied, "No, sir, I was talking to myself." Then he blurted out, "Can I ask you what you meant by what you said about turning back the hands of time?"

"Let me ask you a question first," the man said.

"Okay, go ahead."

"Son, have you ever been in love? Not think you're in love, but in love with a woman. The kind of woman that you believe you can't live without, and you don't want to go one day without being with her."

"Well, no, maybe I have," Rocky stuttered, remembering his girlfriend.

The man continued, "Well, walk with me because I have a story to tell you that you can learn from so you can avoid making the same mistakes I did."

Approaching a bench that was positioned next to the river, the man bid him to sit down. After sitting, the man turned to look at him, as Rocky waited for him to speak.

"Many years ago," he started. "I fell in love with this girl I knew in high school and after dating for a time, we were married. We spent a wonderful life together until one day I got a call. It was the police. My wife had been in an accident and had been taken to the hospital. She lived for a couple more days, then she died. It left me totally heartbroken. Out of curiosity, I looked into what had happened and found out a car had run a red light, broadsiding her. The driver had been trying to make a call on his cellphone, and well you can figure the rest."

Rocky felt bad for the old fellow and looked up in time to see him sniff back a tear.

The man continued, "I was heartsick for a long time, and I didn't think I'd ever get over her death, but I did in time. I knew I had lost the only love I'd ever known, and I never really expected to find a woman to love me like she did. But as time went on, I began looking again hoping to meet one special woman who would set my heart straight again."

Looking at Rocky, the man added, "I dated around but never found any woman I could love like I had before."

Rocky interrupted, "Is this why you're so sad?"

"No," he said, "let me continue. Then it happened. I met this lady, and we dated for a few months, and I thought our relationship was promising. Then without reason, she broke it off, and I haven't seen her since. Unfortunately for me, I was already starting to develop feelings for her. But then she was gone from my life as quickly as she had come."

Again, he hesitated before adding, "Heartsick, I grew desperate for love and started dating one woman after another. I was wild and single and probably would have remained that way if it weren't for the intervention of a co-worker."

"What happened?" Rocky asked.

"As I said, a co-worker approached me one day and asked me the most unusual question I'd ever been asked."

Leaning forward fully enthralled with his story Rocky urged him to continue.

"Well, that co-worker came up to me during lunch and asked me, 'If you were to die today, are you assured that you would go to heaven?' I was taken aback by the question at first.

'How do you mean?' I asked him. "Just what I asked. 'If you were to die today, are you assured that you would go to heaven?' 'To be honest with you,' I told him, 'I'm not sure at all.' 'Well, do you want to be sure?' the co-worker asked me. 'I guess so,' I said. "At that point, he helped me pray the prayer of forgiveness, and I gave my life to Jesus." The old man paused as if to catch his breath.

Feeling frustrated, Rocky asked, "Is this what you wanted to tell me?"

"No, son," the man replied, "I was just setting the groundwork for the rest of my story. Anyway, my co-worker invited me to his church, and I went with him. He introduced me around and I was perfunctory in greeting everyone until I saw this woman. I was introduced to her and found out her name was Sandra, but she preferred to be called Sandy. I will say I was a bit embarrassed because I felt a slight attraction toward her," he said emphatically.

"I'm ashamed to say, I kept going to church partially for my spiritual needs but also to get to know Sandy better. One Sunday, I got up the nerve to ask her out, and she accepted, which made me happy."

Rocky smiled encouragingly.
"To make a long story short," the man said. "We got married."

Rocky noticed a faint smile on the old man as he continued his story. "We were happy for a while, and things were great. I guess I was blind to the inevitable. Slowly we grew apart, and after being married for almost ten years, she decided she wanted out. There was no specific reason except that we had fallen in and out of love during those ten years. I loved her enough to let her go, although it left me with another broken heart."

It took a minute before he went on. "After our divorce, I spent many nights lying awake wondering where it all went wrong. I guess I tortured myself, putting all the blame on me for not doing all I could to make it work. It got so bad that I finally gave up on ever looking for love again. After that, I finally gave up on myself."

He looked sad as he said, "So now you see the results of my decisions. Here I am today, just a lonesome old man who's left with nothing but memories of love and failures."

"Are you okay?" Rocky inquired.

"Not really. Some days I come down by this river just watch the water flow by and ponder the mistakes I've made in my life when it came to loving women." He glanced at the river. "The river's flow reminds me of time and how it flows on through our own lives. It saddens me somewhat to know I've let so much go by without thinking everything through. Regrettably, I refused to climb back up in the saddle one more time for love."

Pausing for a moment, the old man brushed away a solitary tear that had fallen down his cheek. Rocky wondered what this was all leading up to.

Finally, the man spoke again. "Son, a simple lesson of life is to never be afraid of love. Being able to give your love to another is the most precious gift you have to offer."

Rocky started to interrupt, but the old man held his hand up to stop him.

"Let me finish before you speak. I have more I want to say."

"Okay, go ahead," Rocky said.

"Much talk is made about losing love. It's true that if you've put your heart out there and genuinely love someone and your heart gets broken for some reason it hurts really bad sometimes. But you have to learn to overcome the pain and fall in love again. There is nothing this world offers that is better than getting the love of another or giving your love to someone unconditionally. Even if you get your heart broken a hundred times, that number 101 may be the love that you'll remember and enjoy for the rest of your life."

He looked steadily at Rocky. "Now as I look back on it, I wished I would have had someone like me to encourage me to keep looking for love. I didn't. You see the results of that. I've been a lonely old man for many years now, and my time to have someone's love has passed."

Sadness filled his eyes. "But son, you have your whole life ahead of you. I don't want you making the same mistakes I made. Please don't let the past rule you or stop you from seeking love again. Don't let your past have that kind of control over you. It's just not worth it. Besides, think of all you will miss out on. I don't have a single regret except I gave upon love too soon. I will never know what I may have missed out on. This is the one thing I wished I could change," the old man said regretfully.

Rocky sat there next to the old man and didn't quite know what to say to him. Several minutes passed with a thoughtful silence passing back and forth between them.

Suddenly the old man spoke. "Enough about me. I don't know your current situation when it comes to matters of the heart. But I hope you'll take the advice of a lonesome old man and never stop looking for love the rest of your life. I still have my memories of the three different women I shared my heart with, but that's all I have left. For now, those memories have kept me going all these years."

He sniffed back another tear. "It's funny. I can still feel the love I had for each of those women, and it keeps my heart warm when the sky is gray. On days when the sun doesn't shine, that same love lightens up my heart in a wondrous glow, and I remember all the happy times I shared with each one of them."

He turned and looked at Rocky once more. "Son, don't ever give up on love, ever!" He shook Rocky's hand and walked on down the sidewalk that wound along the river.

Rocky sat there dumbfounded and not sure what to think of his encounter with the old man. He watched him until he disappeared from view. As he sat there, he began to remember his own situation and what a mess it was at the moment.

Jumping up, he began walking back to the house where his girlfriend was. He was unsure of what he might be walking back into, but he knew that the old man was right. No fight was worth losing love over.

When he arrived at the house, tempers had cooled considerably. After entering, he found his girlfriend sitting on the sofa. He could tell from the redness around her eyes that she had been crying.

Rocky sat next to her on the sofa. He took her hands in his and said, "Honey, I need to apologize to you for the way I behaved earlier." He reached up and brushed away a solitary tear. "I overreacted by letting my foolish pride get the best of me. I can't tell you how sorry I am for allowing things to get so far out of hand."

He drew her close to him as he wrapped his arms around her. She remained rigid. and he thought it might be over between them, then she began to relax and cuddled up next to him.

As he looked down into her eyes, she lifted her head to press her lips against his. As they kissed, he thought what a fool he had been to nearly throw away the love of this wonderful woman. After what he had heard from the old man, he knew for certain that he was going to heed his advice. He pondered whether he should tell his girlfriend about his encounter with the lonesome old man but thought better of it. No need to "stir the pot" when he didn't have to. They were back together and that's all that matters now.

The next day, Rocky walked back to the bridge half-expecting to bump into that old man again. He was not there where he had met him the day before, so he walked on. Later that night as he lay in bed, he wondered what had happened to that old man. He figured that he would probably never know, but one thing for sure he was going to remember the man's advice. He surmised that what they say about love is true. *It's better to have loved and lost than to never have loved at all! Leastways that's what the old man believed and I guess right now I believe it too.* Rocky thought as he smiled.

Inspiration: I started writing this as a poem, but it just wasn't coming out that way, so I wrote it as a story.

You Can't Go Wrong
C. Holden

Life goes on, I think I heard in a song.

You can't go wrong if you keep your mind strong.

Keep your mind clean and clear and only believe what you hear,

or want to hear.

Because the news will cause you fear,

and the news will give you the blues.

So, wake up and smell the coffee and roses.

Life is not as it poses.

There is always a better day.

So let's look for a better way

and with the dew on the grass in the early morn,

it is time to make bran muffins.

I Do
Donald C. Septer

When we were young and went out to play
Often times it would be just us two
And you would ask me something
Of course I would always say, "I do"

As we grew up and went to school
We attend that school me and you
And when we went out to play
We went out together after I said, "I do"

One day in school you got caught
Passing a note inside your shoe
Although the teacher threw it away
I could read your mind, and I nodded, "I do"

When we finally made it to our teenage years
Something special started to come through
As we began to feel something for each other
You whispered to me, and I knew that "I do"

Off to high school we finally went
And the bond between us grew stronger too
I asked if you would want to go to the prom with me
And of course, you said to me, "I do"

College came along and we parted ways
And being apart sure made me blue
So when spring break came I asked
"Do you still love me?" and you said, "I do"

Graduation came and I could hardly wait
With ring in hand and bended knee in front of you

I asked you for your hand in marriage
And when the preacher asked me, "Do you?"
I said, "Of course I do."

Inspiration: The inspiration for this poem came from the song, "Power of a Love Song" by Tate Stevens. The idea behind this poem was for every circumstance to be answered by the response, "I do."

A barn sketched near Harper, Kansas

Seriously?
Starla Criser

"Mommie! Mommie!" Abigail <u>cried</u> out as she ran into the kitchen. "Come quick!"

Amanda glanced up in mild concern from the stove where she stood stirring <u>chili</u> for the family's dinner. She didn't panic. That hadn't been her four-year-old daughter's cry of pain. No, Abigail tended to yell out loudly whenever she was excited about something and wanted attention.

She set the stirring spoon down and focused on her beloved daughter. "What's up, honey?" Inwardly, she sighed, seeing the snow melting off Abigail's boots onto the freshly cleaned tile floor. She didn't know why she bothered cleaning the floor from the first snowfall of the year until spring. If it wasn't Abigail racing into the kitchen all wet or muddy, it was her seven-year-old twin brothers. Or her husband: the biggest kid of them all.

Abigail shifted from foot to foot impatiently, a tiny frown furrowing her forehead. "Mommie, hurry!"

From outside in the backyard, Amanda heard her sons shrieking in delight, even as they protested, giggling, about Tippy chasing them. What on earth was their ornery <u>pony</u> doing so close to the house? And where was their father?

"Do I even want to ask how Tippy…" She shook her head and turned off the stove. "Get Mommie's coat, sweetheart."

Abigail sped toward the mudroom, her head full of <u>red</u> curls dancing around her bare head. Where was her knitted hat? And where were her matching gloves?

In a flash, her daughter raced back into the kitchen, dragging Amanda's coat behind her, wiping up the trail of snowy water from Abigail's boots. She sighed again but forced a smile as she took the coat.

She barely had it on and was zipping it up when Abigail grabbed the hem of the coat and tried dragging her to the back door.

"Hurry, Mommie! Daddy needs you."

At those words, Amanda's smile of amusement faded. "Is Daddy hurt? Why didn't you tell me that first?" She nudged her suddenly slow-moving daughter into movement.

Abigail cocked her head in confusion as she looked up. "Daddy isn't hurt. He's trying to keep Tippy from smashing Fred."

As they walked outside into the freezing cold, lightly snowing day, Amanda asked, "Who is Fred?"

"Our <u>snowman</u>. He's huge, Mommie!" Abigail spread her arms as wide as they could go and grinned in delight.

She wasn't really surprised. Her kids—and their dad—seemed to name everything. From the family van to his enormous truck, to even the lawnmower.

"Thank the good Lord," Jason called out in relief. "Get hold of Tippy. You and the boys need to get her back to the barn."

Amanda almost asked why the pony was even here but gave up. With her wild bunch, there would be all kinds of excuses. But she couldn't seem to move, gaping at her six-foot-four-inch, muscle-bound husband all but draped in protection over the fattest, tallest snowman she'd ever seen. A snowman with Abigail's knitted hat balanced precariously on Fred's head and her small gloves dangling from two stick arms.

She was about to laugh when all three of her kids began pelting her with snowballs. As she turned to give them all her mother's evil eye—not that they ever cared about it—Tippy trotted over and pushed her down into the six inches of snow face first.

As she came up spitting and grabbing for snow to make a snowball herself, Jason laughed. A hearty laugh that seemed to come clear from his big feet.

So much for "helping" him. She finished her snowball and launched it at him. The snowball war was on!

Inspiration: This was written as part of a writing exercise using the words snowman, chili, pony, cried, *and* red.

Something Smells!
Donald C. Septer

As a young boy, Jim was always getting himself into "situations" that he sometimes needed help to remove himself from. This is the story about one of those "situations" that he found himself in.

He had gone down to the creek to relax and let the day's hindrances float away in the water he was now cooling his feet in. As he sat there, he picked up rocks or little pebbles and tossed them in the water out of sheer boredom.

As Jim sat there lost in the coolness that washed over his feet, something began to "tickle" his nose. He sniffed several short sniffs trying to determine what that smell was and where it could come from. He lifted his feet out of the creek and slipped his shoes on over his wet feet. He could hear a squishing sound coming from his shoes as he moved in the direction of the odor.

As he crested the hill, he saw an exceptionally large tent down below and stopped to survey the layout. He noticed other things like wagons and some smaller tents off to the side. His curiosity got the best of him as he headed down the hill toward the big tent. As he descended, he marveled at all that lay there before him. It only encouraged him to be more curious.

After reaching the bottom of the sloping hill, he walked around and checked out all that was going on. Just then, a <u>clown</u> in full makeup walked by, and Jim finally realized that the smell his nose had picked up belonged to a circus. With a big smile, he continued "snooping" as he went. He heard a noise off to his left and walked over to the wagon with bars on each side. He stopped and sniffed and he thought he knew that smell. And as he approached the wagon, a <u>tiger</u> that had been resting suddenly jumped to his feet and startled Jim with a mighty roar.

He did an about-face and ran as quickly as he could away from the tiger. That's a smell that he was not interested in at all.

When he finally came to a stop, Jim bent over trying to catch his breath. After regaining his nerve, he sniffed the air and found a pleasing aroma floating along, tempting those to come its way. As he rounded another wagon, there it was—the bane of his nose. There was a vendor selling <u>peach</u> pies.

He checked his pockets and pulled out a few coins. After adding up his change, he smiled, since he had enough to make a purchase from the vendor. He paid for the peach pie and had enough coins left over to purchase some <u>grapes</u> as well. Finding a shady spot, he sat down and feasted on his wonderful snack. That pie had never smelled so good, and those grapes were sweet and juicy.

Finished, he rubbed his belly and smiled. After resting for a few minutes more, his curiosity got the better of him again, so he was back on his feet and on the move.

Now Jim found himself in a row of tents where he thought all the "circus freaks" would be on display. As he walked along the row of tents, he would stop long enough to study each tent and what circus freak would be on display to the noisy crowd. At this time of day, each tent was empty of its particular display, so he continued to walk on hoping to at least get a glimpse of one of them. He noticed some movement at the end of the row of tents, so he stopped to watch.

He watched as a man dressed in some kind of strange diaper came out of the tent and set a large basket on the ground in front of the tent, then turned around and went back inside. Jim's curiosity got the best of him yet again as he slowly approached the basket, hoping all the while not to be seen.

He stood a few feet from the basket and studied it for a minute or so. Then he noticed the basket had moved ever so slightly. And he knew in that instant there was something in the basket and he needed to know what it was.

Moving closer, he was within a few inches when he stopped and sniffed. His nose wrinkled at the smell, but he didn't recognize what it was. He was ready to sniff again when the basket moved again, and there came a "<u>hiss</u>." Startled, he jumped back.

At that moment, the man in the white diaper came out of the tent and he hollered at Jim to get away from the basket in an accent he didn't know. He froze on the spot as the man came toward him. The man stopped beside the basket and took the lid off and reached down inside and brought out the largest snake wrapped around his arm that Jim had ever seen. Terror formed on his face as the man said, "Is this what you're looking for?"

Shaking his head 'no', Jim turned and ran in whatever direction showed an open path for him to escape. As he scampered away, the man's laughter echoed in his head.

The next morning, Jim started thinking about what had happened and how lucky he had been to get away. He realized then that letting his curiosity get the best of him was not always a good thing. He learned his lesson that day—not to let his nose get out of joint by sticking it where it didn't belong.

Inspiration: This was written as part of a writing exercise using the words clown, grapes, tiger, hiss, and peach.

His Girls
Starla Criser

What was a good, loving father supposed to do when his wife of six years left him alone with their twin four-year-old daughters for two weeks? Not that Sara was abandoning the family. Her mother in California was having surgery and needed her support. He didn't begrudge her wanting to go. No, he was behind her decision all the way.

But as Jake watched Carie and Casie eating the breakfast of cold cereal that he'd managed to pull together, he felt fear inching through him.

Day one and already he worried he would fail miserably in his first time parenting alone. His girls were adorable and full of curiosity, energy, and, well, mischief. Mostly, he observed these things from a distance. He was a zookeeper specializing in penguin care and training. They lived on his wife's family's farm, but he was far from being a farmer. Yet here he was for his two-week vacation—on a farm, with no penguins around and two red-haired young girls expecting him to keep them safe, loved, and busy.

"Daddy!" Carie yelled with excitement to get his attention. "Daddy, we want to make cookies."

Cookies! That fear budding inside him turned to panic. "Um… we could go into town to the Sugar Lovers Bakery. You always like their cookies."

Casie gave him the same "I can't believe you said that" look their mother was famous for giving him. She added a roll of her green eyes, also like her mother did.

Carie just shook her head, her shoulder-length curly hair swishing around. Reminding him he needed to try to tame their hair into ponytails or something. At least brush it into some sort of tameness. Taking care of penguins was so much easier.

She climbed off the stool at the kitchen island and took off toward where Sara kept the well-worn cookbook she'd inherited from her grandmother. There were so many small colored tabs sticking out, marking favorite recipes, that it was impossible to easily find anything. Maybe his girls would give up.

"Why don't you wait until your mother gets home to make cookies? She loves cooking with you. She…"

Now both girls were shaking their heads, pure stubbornness setting their small chins. "We want to make cookies with you," they said in unison.

"You cook for your penguins," Casie declared.

"So, you can cook with us," Carie added, carrying the cookbook back to the island.

He didn't "cook" for his penguins at the Wildlife Park. He fed them sardines, anchovies, shrimp, and crabs. Not at all the same. And he barely knew how to use the stove, let alone the oven. What if he somehow destroyed Sara's precious stove? His life wouldn't be pretty, that's for sure.

One look at his determined girls, at the eagerness in their eyes, and he knew he'd probably be figuring out how to buy a new stove. He sighed. "Okay."

They bounced up and down, throwing small fists into the air in victory. "Yes! Yes! Yes!"

Although he really didn't want to be doing this, he quietly asked, "What kind are we going to make? Assuming your mother has the right ingredients in the pantry."

"Cherry-ettes," Casie stated, turning pages in the thick cookbook. She couldn't read much more than her name, but that didn't seem to matter. She studied page after page.

Carie wiggled next to her, and both focused on the pages, foreheads pinched in concentration.

He moved behind them, looked down and realized most of the recipes had pictures of the finished product. His wife was a genius!

"Here it is, Daddy!" they squealed together. "Mommie, makes them at Christmastime. We helped her."

They smiled up at him. "We'll help you too," Casie told him confidently.

Jake still would prefer taking them into the bakery, but he said, "Okay, we've got this, ladies."

Their giggles at being called "ladies" had him smiling. He could do this. They could do this.

Fifteen minutes later, he questioned his sanity in agreeing to the cooking session. The island had every measuring cup, every measuring spoon, bowls in various sizes, and ingredients galore covering it. The double ovens were warming. The hand mixer was waiting at the ready. And all three of them had donned aprons. His being his wife's pink one with ruffles, which he hoped his friends never saw him in.

"What's first, Daddy?" Carie asked, kneeling on a stool beside him.

"I puts that paper stuff on the baking sheets," Casie informed him with pride in her voice.

He'd thought they had to grease the sheets, but the girls explained that was "old-school thinking." Clearly this was something their mother had told them. He was glad about that, though.

Jake glanced at the recipe in the open cookbook. "We need the big bowl and the mixer." He pulled the can of shortening closer, along with the

butter, salt, and vanilla. "Carie, we need the powdered sugar. Casie, get the milk from the refrigerator. We're going to blend all of that together."
His girls went into action while he got the right measuring utensils and plugged in the mixer. Then he took another big bowl and measured flour and chopped pecans into it. He was a little concerned about slowing adding that mixture to the creamed mixture. He envisioned a disaster ahead, but he pushed that fear aside. Maybe not. Hopefully not.

When he put the shortening, butter, salt, sugar, vanilla, and milk into the first bowl, he gazed down at it for a second. So far, so good.

Carie scooted next to him and pleaded, "Let me do it, Daddy."

"No, me, Daddy," Casie countered from his other side.

He couldn't see that going well. "I think I'd better do this. You two can make sure I do it right, like your mother would do it."

A couple of minutes later, the mixture looked good. He was almost feeling confident about this project now. Until he reached for the bowl of flour and started adding it. A cloud of flour shot up around them, and he swore, managing to grit out, "Fudgesicles."

His girls were giggling and wiping flour from their faces. He couldn't keep from joining in, but he tried to add smaller amounts of flour with the next addition. A smaller cloud drifted over the bowl this time.

After that, he reviewed the recipe. *Using your hands, form 1-inch balls of dough. Then flatten the balls enough to put a cherry in the middle. Wrap the dough around the cherry and put the balls on the cookie sheet.*

"Cherries. We need to get the cherries out of the bottle," he said, searching the counter for the bottle.

Casie grabbed it and immediately dumped the maraschino cherries into a small bowl. Red juice flew up and splashed onto the white marble countertop. Would it stain? Sara would kill him if it did.

Carie came to the rescue with a roll of paper towels. She tore off several long strips and threw them at him. "Here, Daddy!"

To his relief, the juice absorbed, and there was no apparent staining. He could live another day.

Before he could turn around, Casie was already snagging a small glob of dough from the bowl and trying to make a ball. What a sticky, yucky mess! He so didn't want to be doing this. But when Carie went to work too, he heaved a sigh of resignation and dug into the job as well.

Smashing the balls, adding the cherries, and remaking the balls took some definite skills that he really didn't have. His daughters weren't much better. Still, they managed to get a couple dozen oddly shaped balls onto the cookie sheets. Even though serious bakers might not consider them the pride and joys, he was pretty proud of their accomplishment.

He put the sheets in the ovens and went back to the huge task of cleaning hands, big and small, and cleaning up the countertop. Next came the search through the many kitchen drawers to find potholders to put the cookie sheets on when they came out of the oven. And the search for cooling racks wasn't easy either. For some reason, they were stored on top of the refrigerator. He'd have to ask Sara about that sometime.

While they waited for the cookies to cool and the girls were getting stir-crazy, he decided to call their mother. After checking how his mother-in-law was doing, he said, "You'll never guess what the girls and I just did."

"Put it on speaker, Daddy," Casie ordered, as both girls moved beside him.

Obediently, he did. Sara quickly asked, sounding cautious, "What did you do?"

He couldn't even imagine all the horrible scenarios that must have flashed through her mind. She was well aware of his skills working at the zoo. And his limited skills in dealing with his daughters at home alone. He'd resent her worries, but he understood them.

Before he could answer, the twins burst out, "We made cookies!"

She seemed to suck in a nervous breath before saying, "That's great, Sweeties." She hesitated and added, "Right, Honey? It was great?"

He heard the worry in her tone, bristled a bit. "Yes, we did good."
"We made Cherry-ettes, Mommie," Carie informed with pride in her voice.

"And we had a flour storm, Mommie," Casie tattled, giggling.

"A-a flour storm?" Sara asked, definitely sounding worried.

"Not a big deal," Jake insisted, still picturing the white cloud flying up around them. "Anyway, we cleaned it up." Well, he still needed to clean the floor.

"Wish I'd been there to see it," Sara said, finally sounding amused.

Jake thought about the mess he'd had to clean up and shook his head, even if she couldn't see him doing it. "If you had been here, I wouldn't have been doing this."

"You needed to do this with the girls," Sara told him seriously. "Spend some quality time with them."

Well, he'd be having a lot of "quality time" with them, two weeks' time. It still made him nervous. There was still time for him to screw this up. No! He wouldn't blow this special time with his daughters.

"Sorry, Honey, but we've got to go now. We have to roll the cookie balls in powdered sugar."

"Powdered sugar? Oh, Jake…"

"I've got this," he cut her off. Yes, this would probably create a whole more mess. But they were going to do this.

Already his girls had lost interest in the phone conversation. Casie was reaching for the container of powdered sugar. Carie was getting out clean aprons for them all.

"I need some manly aprons," he muttered as he pulled on another frilly apron, yellow this time.

Sara laughed. "Now I really wish I were there. Get one of the girls to take a picture of you with your phone. They know how."

"Not a chance," he protested, smiling. "You'll just have to envision me yourself."

Carie clearly had heard her mother and reached for his phone. "I knows how to take pictures. Just turn the camera on."

Hesitant but resigned, Jake did as asked before handing her his phone. Casie scurried next to him. Then Carie squeezed beside him and tried to point the phone at all of them. No way could she manage a selfie of them, so he gave in and did it for her.

"Send it to Mommie," they chirped together, dancing in excitement around him.

Again, he did as instructed. A minute later, Sara called back.

"I love it," she said, sounding tearful. "Oh, I miss you all."

"We miss you too," Jake agreed. He looked down at his grinning daughters and smiled. "Okay, we've got to go now. Cookies to finish."

More dancing and bouncing around him. "We'll save you some cookies, Mommie."

"Yes, please." She sounded tearful again.

When she ended the call, Jake looked at his girls, almost seeing mischief building in their eyes. This adventure was no doubt his first trial with them. But to his surprise, he was looking forward to what they came up with next. Maybe being a hands-on father wasn't so hard. Besides, he dealt with slippery, sometimes ornery penguins almost daily.

"Daddy, we want to play dress-up now. Mommie lets us wear her shoes and clothes and…" Casie began.

"Sometimes we wears your shoes," Carie finished.

"We can put on makeup, too. You'd look pretty with blue on your eyes and red on your mouth." Casie pointed to her eyelids in case he didn't understand. Carie touched her mouth.

The fear he'd felt earlier returned with a vengeance. Fear not of failing as a father, but of giving in to those two pairs of excited eyes, two adorable young girls he loved so much.

Money, Money, Money
Don Boldea

Believe it or not, money has always been a problem for me. Oh, I've always made money because I'm a natural born hustler.

For example, my first gig happened when I was only eight years old. I handed out flyers introducing a new Sundries opening in the neighborhood. I convinced the owner that I had the energy to get it done. The owner decided to give me a chance. He would give me a penny for every promotional flyer I put on every neighborhood door. In one day I made my first fifteen dollars. Don't laugh, that's a lot of <u>green</u> for an eight-year-old living in the late fifties.

The owner verified that I didn't just trash the flyers. Unbeknownst to me, he shadowed each previous block to make sure I didn't trash any of the flyers.

I had a few hours before evening closed in so I visited the owner for more flyers. I strolled into the sundry just as the lights came on. He reached into the cash drawer pulled out a crispy new five and ten dollar bill and handed it to me. With a big smile on his face he then asked, "Ready for more?" For three years every summer, Saturday and Sunday I made fifteen dollars.

Every summer until I graduated from high school I sold a farmer's watermelons, corn and pumpkins. During the week I washed dinner dishes for families who went to church on Wednesday night. During the school year I washed the lunchroom dishes for a lunch meal and fifty cents a day.

While I pursued a two year electronic degree I worked for a two way radio shop as a service dispatcher. Next was a stop at Wichita State University. After a boring first semester I left WSU. It was like riding on the back of a <u>turtle</u> through a mushy mud puddle.

Enough is enough is enough <u>talk</u>. Oh, I have made a lot of money, and I certainly have spent a lot of money. I've had a lot of jobs too. They were easy to acquire. During a job interview if I was asked if I think I can do the job described, without a flinch I answer, "Yes I can do that!" Then I'd run home use an encyclopedia and the city library resources to study up on the subject then I'm ready to go for the second interview. Except for a nuclear engineering position, I was usually hired.

I know, I said enough is enough. Are you ready to grab your socks? Here's the real money story.

Every month my wife the CPA balances our home budget debit and credits. There has never been even a penny column out of balance, never. One afternoon during her finance hour all of a sudden I hear this Cinderella meets Frankenstein scream coming from the office.

There's always a first time for everything. Running into the home office I ask, "What's wrong?"

"What's wrong?" She excitedly and loudly says, "There's a $100,000 deposit that has mysteriously found its way into our bank account."

"Honey, now that's funny get it Funny Money," was my comedic comeback.

"No joke, you Dilly Bar come take a look for yourself," she quickly fired back. "This isn't our money."

The immediate reaction was to call the bank and tell them we believe there has been a mistake made in our account. "What do you believe that mistake to be, Mr. Hudson?" the superior sounding voice asked. We explained that a very large deposit was put into our bank account.

After double checking our names, account numbers and our other accounts, the Mr. Arrogant All Mighty reported, "No everything is as it should be according to our records. Our accuracy of records is held to the banking industry's highest standards."

I asked if he could check just one more time.

"Mr. Hudson, I am the Vice President of our prestigious bank and I have a perfect management record. Perhaps you have received an unannounced Estate settlement," he conceitedly responded.

"Can you check that aspect of our question?"

"Even if I would do that, I can't report my finding to you," he once again gave a conceited response.

Fed up with the inability to get satisfaction from the bank we finally visited a lawyer with bank law experience, (The <u>Fireman </u>and Fireman Law Offices). He suggested we obtain a claimant instrument that the bank would have to sign. In short the mystery money's true original owner has no claim to such money regardless of personal, bank, or fiduciary or any other intermediary of said monies.

The bank president's signature was finally inked as well as all other necessary signatures. Ultimately, the bank found their mistake. In good faith the bank did offer us a finder's fee if we returned the total amount of the monies. We had already changed banks and didn't feel any obligation to return the money or accept the finder's fee. The bank's vice president with the perfect management record was no longer employed at the Bank of No Mistakes. Money, Money, Money.
Sometimes, you can't have your <u>cake</u> and eat it too, and then sometimes you can.

Inspiration: This was written as part of a writing exercise using the words fireman, cake, turtle, talk, *and* green.

What the Heck is That?
Starla Criser

"<u>I wanted to eat everything</u> the pretty little lady cooked for me," Austin said to his friend as they sat in their favorite <u>cowboy</u> bar. "You understand. Out of respect. And because I wanted to impress her."

Then he winced, seeing the enormous serving she'd set down in front of him. She'd looked so proud, so adorable. But a glance down at it and his stomach had knotted. "I swear it took my best manners to sit right there in her kitchen and not run for the door."

Tex cocked his head, curious. "But I heard Sally Anne makes the best apple pie in the whole county. Surely…"

"Heard that, too. Was looking forward to it, seeing a nice big one sitting on the nearby counter."

Austin fingered his bottle of beer and shook his head. "Had to get through the first part of the meal, though, to get to that delight."

"So, what was the problem? I've seen you eat almost anything, even that gawd-awful-looking beet salad thing your mom makes."

"Yep, that takes some gumption to swallow it down." He took a swig of beer. "But this casserole… I tell you it nearly made a coward out of me."

"I think you're stretching things. Couldn't a been that bad."

"<u>Blue</u>. Lumpy mess had bluish gravy all over it."

Tex appeared puzzled, brow furrowed. "Blue?"
"Don't quite know how she managed a bluish gravy. Worse than that, though, was her odd combination of meats." He winced again, practically retasting the one and only bite he'd managed to take. "<u>Rabbit</u> and <u>liver</u>."

Tex nearly choked on a sip of beer before chuckling so loud that every cowboy in the bar looked at them.

Austin scowled at them, then more so at his pal. "Thing is, after seeing me struggle not to gag, she gave me the evil eye and took a bite of it off my plate." He remembered how her pretty blue eyes widened in horror. Then she burst into tears.

He grinned. "After we shoved that casserole into the trash, we ate the whole dang pie. Like everyone says, 'best apple pie ever.'"

Inspiration: This was written as part of a writing exercise using the words *cowboy, liver, rabbit, chuckle,* and *blue* in combination with starting off with "*I wanted to eat everything...*"

No Do Overs
Donald C. Septer

Time's a thing that we most abhor
We waste so much and still want more
It's fleeting in moments yet can be a bore
A friend or enemy it's as it was before

We oft think if it was something we could change
But what do we have that we could exchange
We have our lives bound by time as God arranged
To wish that we could change time is just as strange

Would we be willing to give some of our life away
To do something over we done one long ago day
Or would we spend it on time we want to replay
What would there be to give to get God to sway

No, time is our friend or enemy it's up to us
It's really how we use it that creates all this fuss
It's easy to see that more time would be a plus
But I'm afraid it's something God would not discuss

So, we go on in our daily lives struggling against time
When we don't have enough it seems like a crime
We even try to make the best use of it by keeping in rhyme
And think we've done a good job doing it all part-time

But as the sun comes up and slowly rolls across the sky
We watch as time slowly turns and waves us a goodbye
The passing of time is there and its gone awry
Even if we try to ignore it, it still flies by

So, we learn this very important lesson as time rolls over
Seconds, minutes and hours wasted will never be leftovers

We can't change the past, only the future is ours to makeover
Because in life we've learned this one thing, that there's no do overs

Inspiration: I was inspired by the movie, *The Almanac Factor,* which is a time travel movie in which history is changed in people's lives and how they try to change history back.

Hello – Goodbye
Connie Holt

The space between
Is a friendship long,
That only ends at death.
Or a love that's true,
Until it isn't there.
A child who is gone,
Before our time to go.
A newborn eyeing parents.
Then a parent's eyes close forever.
We're all guilty of seldom,
Filling the space with love.

Grandma's Ghost
Donald C. Septer

Grandpa and Mikey were sitting on the sofa watching Grandpa's favorite western TV show when there was a knock on the front door. Grandpa paused the show and told Mikey to wait there on the sofa until he came back. When Grandpa approached the front door, he could see what looked to be two police officers waiting outside in the cold. He reached for the doorknob and twisted it open and pulled the door back. He looked at the two police officers and asked, "May I help you?"

"Are you Arnold Franks?" the older of the two police officers asked.

"Yes, I'm Arnold Franks. Is there something I can help you with?"

"Mr. Franks," stated the older officer, "Do you know an Emma Franks?"

"Why, yes, officer, she's my wife," replied Grandpa.

"Sir," the officer began, "I need you to come downtown with me. We believe your wife died in a tragic accident, which we are currently investigating, and we need for you come with us to identify her remains."

Grandpa staggered a bit at the news before catching himself. "It can't be," he replied. "She left just a while ago to go visit a sick friend and take her some chicken soup. We're watching our grandson Mikey while his parents are out to a company Christmas party. We were waiting for her to return." He hesitated. "Can you tell what happened to her?" asked Grandpa.

"Well, sir," replied the younger officer, "from what we can tell at the crime scene and from our observations, it looks like a reindeer ran her over. We found her face down in the snow with what we believe are reindeer hoof marks all over her back," he finished.

Grandpa sadly shook his head and said, "She was a loving soul and wanted to help her friend although I asked her not to be gone long."

It turned out to be a sad Christmas for all of us, especially Grandpa. He and Grandma had been married for more than fifty years. Now he had to live in the house he and Grandma had shared for many long years; now he was going to live by himself. Days slowly passed. Though the winter days were short, the nights were even longer it seemed.

As the new year began, Grandpa began to tell everyone who would listen about the strange things that were happening in his home. Grandpa stuck to his stories, or tales as some like to call them, but he never wavered about the facts as he remembered them. Things he recalled started the very first morning of the new year. Grandpa said, "I got up that morning and as I sat on the edge of the bed, I swore I could smell the scent of fresh coffee in the air."

Grandpa's eyes widened as he continued, "When I got downstairs to the kitchen, there was a fresh pot of coffee waiting on the counter, which I assumed was for me. What's crazy is that I don't drink coffee!"

People turned away so Grandpa wouldn't see them laughing and snickering at his wild tales.

"That ain't all," he continued. "At night after I go to bed, I swear I hear the vacuum cleaner running in the living room, but by the time I get downstairs to find out what is going on, it's all quiet." More turned heads accompanied by laughs or giggles. "Laugh all you want, but I know what I heard," he said.

Mikey didn't like the way people laughed at his grandpa because he thought it was cruel to laugh and make fun of someone who had recently lost his wife. Mikey decided he was going to show them, so he decided he would spend the weekend with his grandpa and prove to the town folks that they were wrong for making fun of his grandpa.

In the early hours of Saturday morning, Grandpa woke up Mikey and told him to listen and breathe in that smell. Mikey listened and breathed in the wonderful aroma that permeated the upstairs. Grandpa looked at Mikey and said, "See, what I told you. Now that you can hear and smell for yourself, I know you can show up all those people who think I'm crazy."

Grandpa stood up and motioned to Mikey to follow him quietly toward the stairs that led down to the kitchen. "Grandpa," Mikey said, "That smells like Grandma's biscuits and gravy. I can smell bacon cooking as well."

"Shhh," Grandpa shushed, "Be quiet." Then he motioned with his hand to Mikey to follow him. Quiet as possible, they both crept down the stairs toward the kitchen. Standing outside the kitchen, Grandpa whispered, "Ready? Go." With that they both burst through the kitchen door to find a room full of nothing but silence.

Finally, the day came that drove Grandpa from his home permanently. It had been nearly a year since a reindeer had run Grandma over, and the anniversary was only a few days away. He had gone to bed "with the chickens" as usual. He was snuggled in bed for the night and had fallen sound asleep when something on the roof woke him up. Through sleepy eyes, he tried to comprehend what was going on. Then he heard it again, and he became fully awake. Up on the roof, he heard what he determined were reindeer hooves. Suddenly, an image he swore was Grandma, appeared and floated above his bed.

It was as if Grandpa became a bolt of lightning. He jumped out of bed and pulled on his clothes and grabbed his coat and was quickly on his way out the front door. He ran all the way over to where Mikey lived with his parents and stood there beating on the front door until his son let him in. He was shaking as he related what he had seen. Mikey's parents had a difficult time believing him, but he refused to ever go back to that house again.

It took Grandpa a few days to find him a small apartment on the other side of town from where he used to live. Mikey's parents had gone in and packed all his belongings and moved him out of the house. It took a couple of months before new owners purchased Grandpa's home. It wasn't long before the new owners started getting "visits" from Grandma's ghost. A month after they moved in, they put the house up for sale. The story around town that was told over and over again by everyone was that they had seen Grandma's ghost riding a reindeer throughout the house. Most town folk got a big laugh out of their story.

Although people around town swear, they have seen Grandma's ghost leading around a reindeer apparition. Those in town who never saw what the others did would laugh and make fun of them when they were told. "Well, they can laugh all they want because it doesn't matter anymore," Mikey said. "They can say that there is no such thing as ghosts, but as for me and Grandpa, we believe!"

Inspiration: This was written as a writing exercise. The exercise was to pick a Christmas song title and write a story from it. I chose, "Grandma Got Run Over By a Reindeer."

Life Goes On
C. Holden

We have climbed mountains together

Crossed many swollen streams

Chased a lot of rainbows and dreams

Now that we are getting older

We still have each other

And life goes on.

Camp'n In the South
Tom Elman

"Hey ya'll. Let's go camp'n this weekend." Bobby Bob Roberts stood there with his left hand stuck down inside the slit in his coveralls. His three-tooth smile was from ear to ear. And he had his right index finger searching for treasures in his nose.

Missy Mae Roberts jumped up and down on the sofa. "That sounds like a lotta fun, Unkka Bobby. Where ya wanna go?"

"Maybe all the way out to the other side of our back fence."

"Land sakes, Bobby, it would take us half a day to lug all our camp'n stuff back thar. Why cain't we'uns just hook up a tarp to our lean-to tween Jeannie Joe June's lean-to and Andy Aloyishus Argile's lean-to and have us a picnic right here?" Billie Bobbie Roberts looked over at her husband Bobby Bob and threw her hands in the air and then smacked her right hand with a 'Blam' on the kitchen table (which, by the way, once was a wire cable spool from when the government boys brought electricity to their holler). "That fly ain't neva go'n ta laund in my chitlins again."

"Geez! Billie Bobbie, Ah jest thinked you'd like ta git away from this place for a little while and enjoy some new scenery."

"Bobby Bob, I can see the danged back fence from right here."

"Ah, Mom! Let's do it like Pappy sez. It will be fun way out there. I ain't never been on the othah side ah that fence."

"Billy Binky Bobby, what do you mean 'way out there'? Don't you remember that one day when you was thirteen, and we sent you off to kindygarten? You was gone for three days before you found your way back home. And I don't think you wooda ever found your back if it twernt fo ole Blue sniff'n ya out from under Jeremiah Finch's woodpile next to his outhouse. That was four houses down the path from here."

"Geez, Momma, that were at least ten years ago. I think it's time for me to venture out again."

"Yeah, Momma, Billy Binky Bobby is right. And I be speak'n for Billie Barbie, Billie Bonnie, Billie Bettie, and Ralphy. We all wanna go camp'n cross the fence. Billy Binky Bobby, stop eat'n them ants. Momma, make him stop."

"You're right, Jenny Jo Jean. Billy Binky Bobby! Stop eat'n them ants like your sister say."

"That settles it. We all gonna go camp'n onna othah sidda the fence. Andy Aloyishus Argile, you get the canoe and tote it out to the back fence."

"Poppa, they ain't no water back there."

"It might rain, and you know how fast that crick fills up. Now git out there and do what I told ya, boy."

"I'm on it, Poppa. Can I take Ralphy ta hep."

"For cry'n out loud, he's only three … or maybe five years old."

"But he's a strong un, Poppa."

"Well, okay. And you gals give yo momma some help loading up the vittals. And don't ya'all forget ta bring that sack of popcorn. Kain't go camp'n without popcorn."
"And Bobby Bob, don't you forget ta take your bi-nocks so'as tonight we can all see what the moon looks like from way out yonder."

"Bobby Bob. When those nosy neighbors of ar'n see us'n out there, I know they'z gonna be write'n this camp'n trip up in the *Daily Shopper*. You just wait and see."

The Field Trip
Starla Criser

The school year had just started, and already Susan's class was taking a field trip to the zoo. On an afternoon that was nearing 90 degrees. She'd been hot from the second they left the elementary school. Hotter as her treasured first graders crowded onto the bus. Plus, her students were excited, wiggling in their seats.

She swiped at the sweat beading on her brow. Smiled her best for the adorable kids that couldn't wait to get to the zoo. Neither could she.

"Everybody buckled in?" the middle-aged, balding bus driver <u>yelled</u>.

Susan walked up and down the aisle, checking to be certain each of the twenty-five kids had fastened their seatbelts. It looked like they were good to go. She sighed in relief and nodded back at the driver before heading for her seat at the front.

"<u>Teacher</u>," Abigail said and snagged Susan's hand as she started by the cute little blonde. "Sit with me. Please."

The poor girl looked worried. For most of these children, they'd never been on a school bus before. Most were happily anticipating the adventure. A couple, Abigail in particular, not so much.

Susan gave a reassuring smile and eased into the window seat beside the girl in the <u>white</u> T-shirt with a picture of a <u>penguin</u> on it.

"Thanks," Abigail said in a small voice.

"I like your shirt," Susan said, hoping to lighten the moment. "Are you looking forward to seeing the penguin exhibit?"

Abigail's eyes brightened, and she reached into the pocket of her shorts. Glancing around to see if anyone else was watching, she pulled out her hand, something clasped tightly between her small fingers.

"What do you have there?" Susan asked, curious about what was evidently a secret.

Abigail worried her lower lip for a second, then leaned closer to Susan. She opened her fist to reveal tiny pieces of crushed <u>bacon</u>. "Mom doesn't know I snuck these off my breakfast plate this morning."

"Ummm. Why do you have pieces of bacon?" They were planning to eat lunch at the zoo. Surely Abigail didn't think she needed to bring along a snack too.

"They're for the penguins." Abigail whispered. "I wanted to bring them something special."

Uh-oh. How did she not upset the cute little girl who just wanted to share with her favorite animals? "I don't think the zookeepers will let us feed them, honey."

"But they let me feed the giraffes sometimes," Abigail protested, clearly confused.

Toby, sitting across the aisle, a sweet little boy who had become one of Abigail's classroom buddies, shook his head at her. "Penguins don't eat bacon, Abby."

Her forehead creased, and she looked from her precious bacon bits to her friend. "Are you sure? Everyone likes bacon."

His small shoulders slumped, as if afraid of hurting her feelings. After a glance at me, he shook his head and said, "Not me, Abby. I don't like bacon." He looked at me again before adding, "My dad says penguins eat fish."

"Really?" Abigail asked, puzzled. "Okay, more for me." Then she shrugged, smiled, and tossed the bacon bits into her mouth.

Wiping off her mouth with the back of her hand, she looked up at me, hope in her expression. "Will they let me feed them fish?"

"The zookeepers will feed them, Abby," Toby explained. "We get to watch them do it."

Susan wasn't sure what to say, but Abigail simply said, "Oh, okay."

Inspiration: This was written as part of a writing exercise using the words teacher, bacon, penguin, yell, *and* white.

For Old Glory
Donald C. Septer

As I lay here waiting for death to make me still,
I fight to live with my full-hearted will,
My body's broken and ravaged by this war,
Because I gave my all fighting for the Army Corps.

What did I have to gain with so much to lose,
I guess I always knew and that I didn't have to choose,
For old glory waved and called me to the battlefield,
And when the red, white and blue called I wasn't about to yield.

I was proud to serve and answer freedom's call,
And I'm still willing to give it my all in all,
I know the truth about what freedom costs,
And all about the lives that were given and lost.

I've listened to those who say two wrongs don't make it right,
That the cost we have to pay is not worth the fight,
They've all said I'm misguided, and war is not the way,
But I stood tall and looked at them and this is what I had to say.

"Freedom isn't free and it will never be,
And if you'd only open your eyes then you just might see,
That no sign crying 'peace' or 'make love and not war',
Made an enemy give up and cry out for 'no more'."

"But it takes the blood and sweat of our fighting men,
Giving their lives to bring all war to a bitter end,

You see this country is envied for just this one thing,
And that's because we allow our freedom to ring."
"You're allowed to do and say anything you want,
Because of the soldiers who've died at the battle front,
So, leave me alone because you won't ever change my mind,

And I sure won't listen to those I think are so blind."

"So, I'm leaving it in God's hands as to whether I live or die,
I'll always believe its better to go this way than to say I didn't try,
For the truth about freedom has but one simple story,
And it can only be told by those who have fought and died for old glory."

Inspiration: I wrote this poem to add to my Vietnam book. In the poem, I tried to show how a patriotic soldier felt about serving his country.

The Magic of Love
Donald C. Septer

Chapter One: Magic Midnight

"Love is better the second time around," Michael heard Luther's sweet voice sing through the speakers of his stereo. *I sure hope so*, he thought as he watched his reflection of shaving in the mirror. His mind again drifted off to Becky, *I sure thought we had something special going on, but what can I say? Sometimes what can look so good at first can end up being so bad inside.*

I'm not saying what we had was all that bad, he thought. *But it had burned out so quickly that both of us were caught unaware that we had fallen out of love with each other. When it came time for us to break up*, he mused. *I think we both knew it was over. Just a mutual agreement to go our own separate ways, no fanfare, no funeral, we just agreed to let it end.* He frowned.

After dressing and grabbing a quick bite to eat, Michael headed off to work. It was time to make a living. He wasn't sure what it was, but from the moment he got in his refurbished '66 Mustang to head for work he could feel a strange wind blowing in the air. All day long, through the long hours, something stirred at his soul.

After work, he was happy to have the day over as he headed home. After eating a hastily thrown together meal, he sat back in his easy chair, picked up the newspaper TV guide to check out his night's viewing. He began scanning the guide on the page, hoping something would grab his attention.

There hadn't been much to choose from as most what he saw were reruns, which held little interest to him. Disgusted with the fare, Michael picked up the remote so he could do a little "channel surfing" so that he could check all the channels not listed in the newspaper TV guide. Unfortunately for him, he found nothing worth viewing and he sure wasn't interested in watching any sports event, so he decided to shut the television off.

For some reason, he felt restless tonight, but he couldn't put his finger on what was eating at him. He thought he'd just go out for a walk and maybe that would clear his head. It was possible that after a quiet walk in the night he could get a good night's sleep when he got back.

Closing the door behind him, he stood there wondering which way to go. An impulse hit him with the urge to take a walk along the river that was several blocks away. Since he had nothing better to do, he thought, "What the heck," and headed in that direction. Something about his decision seemed to lift his spirits in a way that was mystifying yet comforting.

As Michael walked toward the river, memories of Becky drifted back into his mind. Flashes of their times together appeared and dissolved away as quickly as they had come, somewhat like their relationship. He thought it best if he just cleared his mind of all the "noise" and walked along in the night's solitude.

Though in the dark, he had somehow stumbled onto a jogger's path that ran parallel to the river and began walking. Checking his watch for the time, he saw that it was 9:15 p.m. and thought he'd walk along for about 45 minutes then walk back home hoping he'd be tired enough for a good night's sleep.

As he walked, Michael was surprised when he came across a bench that sat alongside the pathway. He noticed the bench faced the river, so he sat down to take a load off. As he sat there watching the river drift slowly by, he began to nod off. Leaning back, he closed his eyes to listen to the night. Hypnotized by the soft sounds of the night, he drifted off to sleep.

A wild animal screeched, jolting him awake, and had him glancing at his watch to check and see how long he had been sleeping there on that bench. His watch glowed back at him saying that it was 11:45 p.m. He arose quickly to leave and realized he hadn't finished the walk he had planned. He started back in the direction he thought he had come. *If I take a quick walk in the other direction I could come up about 3 blocks from my home, and it would be closer than going back the way I came.* He knew after that nap he would now need to exhaust some restored energy to be tired enough to go to sleep when he arrived home.

Trotting along the riverbank, Michael found himself draggin' his thoughts along in the water. Lost in thoughts of the past, he glanced up at the midnight moon and without much thought he noticed there seemed to be something magical about it. Something in the air raised goose bumps on his arms. He looked up at the moon again only to be surprised because he thought it had winked at him. He shook his head and thought he'd better get home.

Across the river, he noticed the city lights were growing hazy. He hadn't noticed that the lights had started to dim when he started back. Now they were being blotted out by an eerie misty haze. It was getting hard for him to see, so he thought it wise to be more cautious as he made his way back home. As he walked, he carefully focused on what lay before each step that he took. Hesitantly, he continued to wade through the magic mist that caressed his feet.

Suddenly something brushed past him, startling him, which caused him to jump. Looking around and not seeing anything, he assumed that it had been his imagination. *No, it must have been something caught up and blown by the wind.* Unnervingly, an aching chill raked through his entire body as a touch of fear glanced through his senses.

As if by magic, there she stood in front of him, standing just out of reach. Surprised, Michael was taken aback by her sudden appearance. At first glance, he thought he was seeing a ghost, so he shook his head trying to clear his thoughts.

Silently, she moved swiftly toward him as if she were floating on a cloud, yet everything seemed to move in slow motion. He muttered to himself that this was nothing more than a dream and that he was safely at home and in bed.

Frightened by her sudden appearance, he closed his eyes in fear of what would happen next. He waited for what seemed an eternity, and nothing happened. Timidly, he opened his eyes to find her standing in front of him, practically face to face. Something about her drew him to her like a magnet; he swore he was falling under some kind of spell. For reasons unknown, he couldn't break eye contact with her as he gazed into the magical mystery in her eyes.

He felt like he was caught up inside of a whirlwind and that his entire body was floating, lost in the magical mist that swirled around inside his head. Through it all, he sensed that something was tingling at his nose. And he knew in that moment he could smell the scent of love as it filtered throughout his fog-bound mind. Adrift in his own world, he felt the touch of something soft and warm against his lips. Somehow, he knew that it was her welcoming and tantalizing lips that were pressing against his. Her kiss was sweet and tasted like nothing he had ever experienced before.

He sensed a deeper, delicious kiss, and it made him feel like he was in a dream. He could hear his heart screaming, "Don't stop, don't stop."

As her lips gently released their touch on his, he opened his eyes only to see a multicolored mist swirling in the spot where she had just stood. Michael's heart sank from the elation it had momentarily felt. Sadly, he bowed his head and slowly made his way back to where the pathway led him home. After relishing the touch and soft desire from her lips, he was so downhearted that he never realized how late it had gotten. Heading home, he scuffed his heels as he walked.

Chapter Two: Another Magic Midnight

Several weeks passed since that night, but the thought of what had happened never left Michael's mind. *Wished I had thought to ask her what her name was.* However, he had a gut feeling that it never really happened and that it had been nothing more than a dream. Still, he had a sensation on his lips that refused to go away. But the strangest thing of all was that every time he'd run his tongue over his lips, he swore he could taste a sweetness that was akin to honey.

Friday night finally arrived, dragging with it the weekend and he was sure glad when five o'clock arrived. He closed the door to his office and walked down the hall and out to his "stang" and got in. Turning right out of the driveway, he headed north on Holly Avenue in the direction of his bank. After picking up some cash for the weekend, he drove home with thoughts of her on his mind.

After supper, he settled down in his easy chair and picked up the TV control and began channel surfing. As before, the same old shows he had seen over and over were all that seemed to be on the TV's schedule. He had had enough of that, so he shut the TV off and settled back in his easy chair for some shuteye. With all the lights out, it seemed so quiet that all he heard was the ticking of the clock that felt like it was keeping perfect time with the beating of his heart.

Ignoring that, he closed his eyes and listened to the sounds the house was making. He listened to each sound, hoping he would drift off to sleep. Unfortunately, it was impossible as the sound of his heartbeat kept invading his hearing.

He sat there in the growing darkness, watching the shadows of dying sunlight fade to black until the only light in the house came from the streetlight that was outside in his front yard. He sat and watched the reflection of lights flashing across the walls of his living room as each car passed by going down the street. The weariness of his past week's work weighed on him as he wanted to relax but was unsuccessful.

Something struck a "chord" in him that made Michael sit up with a start. *Why not go see if I can find her again.* He knew deep down inside that he had to determine if she was real or if she had been a figment of his dreams and inner desires. He decided the only way to find out was to go back down to the river and search for her and hope that he might "bump" into her again.

He decided this time to drive down to the river instead of walking. That way, if he did "accidentally" meet her, he could at least offer her a ride home. *That way I can find out where she lives and maybe ask her out.* As he drove the three blocks toward the river, he became apprehensive about seeing her again. Regardless, he was still looking forward to another "chance" meeting with her. That gnawing feeling he had in his gut wouldn't go, and it caused him to feel like he was on a wild goose chase as he couldn't be that fortunate to find her again.

Upon arriving at the river, he glanced at his watch and saw that it was only 9:37 p.m. It wasn't that late, so he decided that he would do his best and not take any chances. He had met her there once, and he was going to go back to that same place hoping for another "chance encounter." His reasonable thinking brought him back to the place he had met her before. Looking both ways, up and down the river, he walked upstream. After he had been walking for a while, he still hadn't encountered anyone. Disappointed, he was ready to give up when the idea of finding the bench he had been on and waiting there for her struck him. He wandered around for close to 20 minutes before he found it. Smiling to himself, he sat down to wait.

As Michael sat there, he thought back to that "magic" midnight when he had first met her. The mystery that surrounded their meeting washed across his thoughts like a gentle breeze on a summer afternoon. He remembered thinking that she was a ghost and how frightened he had been at first. Then the softness of her lips against his and that taste of her honey sweet breath was so intoxicating to his senses that he felt weak in his knees, and he was glad that he was already sitting down.

He snickered to himself. "I might have fainted on the ground if I hadn't been sitting here on this bench." What bothered him the most was the sadness he felt when she left him without saying a word. His chance meeting with her had left him with more questions than answers, but he felt that if he by "chance" would happen to see her again he was hopeful he would be able get the answers to some or all his questions.

Lost in thought, he slowly let his head sag back and drifted off to sleep again. As he slept, images of her filled his dreams. He could see himself stumbling along in the dark trying to find his way back to her. He watched himself leave the bench and stumble around trying to find the spot where he had met her. In his dream, he had a déjà vu moment as he encountered the sense that he had been here before. "Yes!" His heart cried out. "This is it, the place where he had felt the warmth of her kiss." He thought he was in heaven, floating on a cloud from his euphoria.

An eerie chill awakened him, stroked his spine, as he felt a light tap on his shoulder. Though fear gripped him, he sensed a calmness about him as he slowly looked up, curious to see who had awakened him from his dreams. There she stood as though she had leaped out of his dream and into his reality. Once again, she wore a slight pixie smile, and that somehow made him feel at ease.

As he started to speak, she pressed her index finger to his lips and shook her head "no." In a loving manner, she reached down and took Michael's hand and drew him up next to her and started pulling him to follow her down the path that ran along the river. He felt like a giddy child at the elation of her touch and her hand in his.

He lost track of everything around him as he believed that time was standing still for the two of them. The few short minutes they walked felt as they had lasted a lifetime. He knew he would love to endure the endless hours left in his life if he could spend them locked in this very moment.

Suddenly, without warning, she stopped and pulled his arms around her tight and gazed into his eyes with a look that was pure magic. He stood there stunned, unable to move a muscle, not knowing what to do or expect. Their lips joined in a kiss as he lost himself in their passion. Without warning, everything went black as he crumpled to the ground.

The light of a new day filtered through the throbbing ache in his head. He felt achy all over. He tried to focus his sandpapered eyes as he picked himself up off the ground. After getting on his feet, his entire body shivered from lying on the cold ground. In the growing daylight, his head began to clear, and for the first time he realized he was alone…again.

Staggering back to his car, he climbed in and fumbled through his pockets for his keys. Irritated, he jammed the key into the ignition switch. He fired up his Mustang, backed it up and headed the car back toward his home. After pulling into the driveway, he shut the car off, got out, went inside and closed the door behind him.

Still shaking, he undressed and got in a warmer than usual shower to rinse out the cold he felt from his night on the ground. After toweling off, he stretched out across his bed and began to relive the events of the previous night. Once again, he was left with a puzzle that he could not solve. *Did he just fall asleep on the bench again and just roll off onto the ground, or did what he remembered, really happen?* His fog-choked mind was no help as he could not discern the fantasy from the reality.

Restlessly, he arose and pulled the covers down and climbed into bed to take the chill off and get some needed rest. As he lay there, the dryness of his throat caused him to lick his lips. As the taste of honey began to filter through his senses, he found he could not stop his smile.

Chapter 3: Final Magic

Days passed since that second night. Michael had searched and dreamed, trying to bring her back, but nothing he tried would solve his plight. Several times he had gone back to the river, but nothing. He even waited several nights until well after midnight and still nothing.

Michael realized it was over and that he needed to get on with his life. He could never prove to himself one way or another whether she was real or just an apparition of his imagination. Regardless, he had to push the thoughts of her out of his mind and the feeling out of his heart and just get on with his life.

Often, as the days passed, he would find his thoughts floating back to her. Fortunately for him, with the passing of time he found himself thinking less and less of her. He started dating again to relieve the ache in his heart and found that with each date the pain he felt would lessen. He was beginning to enjoy the company of a woman again.

He had dated a variety of women but kept in mind the kind of woman that he wanted to have a future with. He dated around without having much luck finding any woman that he would consider even wanting a relationship with.

After several months, Michael was able to put her memory in the past where she belonged. He was looking forward to the day when he would finally meet that certain someone who would bring that "love" that would satisfy his heart for the rest of their lives.

He had realized that if he kept searching, he would eventually find the one. And when she came into his life, he would know in an instant that she was right for him. He knew he would find the one who had love in her heart and that it would be true and kind but, most of all, she would be his.

To make sure that he would be successful in eradicating her memory from his mind, he threw himself into his work. He did whatever he thought would keep his mind off her. Days passed, and so did her memory. He was getting on with his life, and he was happy again.

Then, without notice, her memory pulled so strongly on his heart that it seemed to demand that he go back to that very spot where they had first met. Deep inside him, he felt that this was where he needed to be, down by the river, letting his feet dangle in the cool water. Hard as he tried fighting it, the feeling wouldn't go away. He battled the desire for several days but found himself on the losing end of the struggle.

As Michael neared the spot, he noticed someone standing next to the bench. Although the sun was beating down hot on her, it was as if she didn't have a care in the world. All kinds of thoughts rushed through his mind: *Was it her, is this the one who I met during those magical nights?* His heart leaped and bounded. *What if it is her? My search would be over. How lucky can one guy be?*

Standing as if he were glued to one spot, he watched as she turned around so that he might gaze upon her loving face. His heart dropped and his soul realized that it was not her. Though he could only remember a few ghostly images of her face, he knew that *she* was not the one he was looking for.

Then something about her caught his eye. Boldly, without realizing what he was doing, Michael began walking toward her. Something seemed to draw him to her. He hadn't realized what he was doing because it was totally out of character for him. As he drew nearer to her, she smiled a smile that reached inside his chest to disturb his heart.

As the distance had closed between them, it seemed as if sparks had flown, and he knew he had to kiss her. He knew it was something he was being driven to do. Suddenly he stopped as they stood face to face. Totally absorbed in their closeness, they both seemed unaware of their surroundings. Not a word was spoken, but their hearts seemed to speak volumes to each other. Everything remained in its place. It was as though destiny had brought them together at this very moment.

Without a word spoken between them, they embraced each other and found themselves locked in a kiss so full of passions that he swore it colored the sky rainbow shades of purple. He thought of nothing but the kiss he was sharing with this stranger. His mind reeled as if what they were sharing was filling the emptiness that he had grown to know.

As their lips parted, Michael stepped back embarrassed by his actions. Tongue-tied, he could not find the words that would describe to her his embarrassment for what he had done. He tried to convince himself that she wanted it as bad as he did, but that was a foolish thought. He knew that any second, she would probably slap him and start screaming that he had assaulted her and he was going to have much to explain.

Something in her eyes captured his attention, and there in the light of day his heart recognized something that his mind had not seen. He saw a smile form on her lips, so he smiled back. Just then, she reached out and took his hand in hers. Much to his surprise, she began to urge him to walk with her.

As they walked, he searched his mind for the right words to say to her. But for some inexplicable reason he was at a loss for words. Silently, they walked together. Only the sounds of nature made their way into their little world. They walked hand in hand for a while, stealing glances at each other. The world seemed to be open to both.

Michael's imagination ran wild and without realizing it, he had developed a thirst and absent-mindedly licked his lips. He stopped to speak and before he could utter a word, a familiar taste caressed his mouth. But his mind was puzzled at what it could be. "I know that taste," his mind screamed.

The silence between them was strange indeed. He was perplexed at what she might be thinking, but here he was walking with a stranger whom he had just walked right up to and embraced and kissed without any introduction and never apologized for his forward behavior. *What is so strange*, he thought, *is that it didn't seem to bother her at all.* All he knew was that their actions seemed to fulfill the needs in his heart.

As they continued their walk, he figured out the answer to the puzzle his mind had struggled to solve. He finally figured out what that taste was. Quickly he stopped and pulled her close, he knew that he had to know for sure. Once again, they joined in a long, passionate kiss that left his head spinning.

As he stepped back, he inhaled a sweet odor that blazed through his senses, and he realized in that moment it was her perfume. The scent was so tantalizing that he had to know. Looking deep inside her mesmerizing eyes, he asked, "What is that wonderful perfume you're wearing?"

With a smile that held the answer to every question he had, she smiled. In that moment his heart, his mind, his body and his soul knew without a doubt *this* was the woman that would be his love of a lifetime, when she spoke those two words.

With a hint of mischief, she said, "Magic Midnight."

Inspiration: I originally wrote three poems which I used as chapter titles. I liked the poems so much I fleshed them out into a story.

The Haysville Rest Home/Round-up Rodeo
Anonymous

Ron and Rex are very able clinicians at the local seniors' rest home. They were just finishing their morning coffee. They both knew that this was going to be a very strenuous day for them.

Ron looked over at Rex. "We better get our best acts together today."

Rex nodded to Ron. "We're going to need our best gears to keep this bunch in line."

"It's going to be a real challenge to get all these old codgers from here to the auditorium by 10 a.m.," said Ron.

Rex shook his head and smiled at Ron. "I know! I know! This could be a serious problem seeing that it's 7:30 now, and it's over 100 yards from here to the auditorium."

"I know, Rex. So, let's get over there and get started. The headman says, 'we' got to do this because no one else is capable."

They entered the unit and rang the bell. "Roing it again, Ron."

Rex shouted, "Alrighty! All you deadheads, get out of bed and get dressed as fast as possible."

Rex stood on a chair and yelled, "Who needs to get to the hospital? The ambulance is parked out front. And, Bessie, I said 'hospital' not 'popsicle.'"

Ron shouted again, "We're all going to the corral. Oops! I meant the auditorium for the best show of the year."
Mable looked at Rex and said, "You say it's going to snow on my car in the auditorium?"

"No, Mable! I said it's going to be the Show of the Year."

"Well, I'm going to take my shawl to keep from freezing," said Mable.

"Ron! Get over here quick. You need to get Frank out from under his bed. I've got to get Wayne. He's gone and locked himself in the women's bathroom. Again!"

Rex started guiding Maggie, George, Mable, and Bessie toward the door. "Let's get a move on, you little doggies. We've got to get you all over to the auditorium for all the goodies and treats."

Bessie grabbed his arm. "Oh no, Rexie, I'm afraid of those hoodies on the streets."

Rex put his hand on her shoulder. "There aren't going to be any hoodies. We're just going across the parking lot to the show."

Maggie put her hand on Rex's arm. "Can we feed some of the treats to the pigeons when we get to the park?"

Rex looked Maggie over. "Yes! Sure! Now, turn your dress around and find someone to help you with the buttons."

"Hey, Rex. Good herding start. Keep moving them toward the door. Dammit, Frank's back under his bed again."

Rex is ushering most if the folks toward the door. Ron is rounding up the last of the strays.

"I sure hope we don't see any yellow snow on the way."
"Mable, I told you before it's not going to snow and put your other shoe on and let's go."

Ron stops everyone at the door. "Hey! Everybody! They are going to serve crepes as soon as we get inside."

"Oh goody! I love grapes, but they get stuck in me on the way down."

"You don't have to eat any grapes, Alice. Oh, by the way, why did you bring your suitcase?"

"Ron, you said we were going to the hospital."

"Oyvey1"

"Rex, keep them together. Keep an eye on George. He made a run for the fountain the last time we tried this."

INSIDE:

"May I have your attention," blasted out of all the speakers. "Please! Welcome to the annual Haysville Rest Home/Round-up Rodeo."

"Did he say there was going to be an arrest announcement on the radio?"

"No, Mable. He said we are all welcome to the rodeo. Now you get over there and get something to eat before the games start." Ron and Rex looked at each other and just smiled.

The speakers blasted again, "Your attention, please. Please! The first round-up rodeo event will be the famous bedpan relay. Now, pick your partner and mosey over to the starting line, where Ron and Rex are standing. Every team has a bedpan.

"George! Give me that punch bowl you took from the lunch table." Ron put the punch bowl back on the table.

"The rules. The first racer runs with his pan to the other side of the floor. He or she fills the bedpan and then runs back across to their partner. The partner empties the pan and then runs to the other side of the floor. Fills the bedpan and runs it back to the finish line. First team back wins two full cases of Depends."

"Ron?"

"Yes, Alice?"

"Can I use a walker?"

Speaker blasts, "Runners, to your marks. Go!"

"Come on, Mable. One foot in front of the other."

Rex nudges Ron. "Did you know Mable has a prosthetic leg?"

Ron cheers, "Hop! Mable! Hop!"

"Rex, I'm going across the floor to make sure nobody cheats."

Ron stays around the fill-up area. "Come on, George, you're almost to the wall. That's close enough. Start filling."

Ron keeps an eye on George. "What's wrong, George? Nothing? Oh! Just keep trying as hard as you can."

"Bear down, Maggie, it'll come."

"Stop holding your breath, Alice." Your face is turning purple."
"Ok! George, that's a start."

"Way to go, Maggie. Even with that poor start, you managed to get it topped off. Now quit, Maggie. No more! That's enough."

"Hee, hee, hee, Ron. I just can't stop."

Ron started looking for a mop and bucket.

Rex came over to help.

"George, get up. Stop rolling in that wet stuff."

"Hey, Ron, they're starting to stampede."

Rex is afraid.

"Gadzukes, Rex! I'm getting out of here."

Rex. "Me too!"

CONTRIBUTOR LIST